Welcome to Laurel Oaks Plantation.
I'm frightfully glad you're here.

- Do not attempt to enter the General Cambridge Suite at the far end of the gallery.
- The golden key opens the door at the bottom of the steep staircase leading to the dark belly of the house.
  BEWARE THE TWELFTH STEP.
- Keys wait in the doors of your rooms at the top of the stairs. The Eberly room is on your right; the Brookes and Gladstone rooms are on your left. Choose wisely.
- Caution: **Do not, DO NOT *turn out the light in the hall.* When the last light at Laurel Oaks is snuffed out, the spirits are released to take their pleasure.
- There are no phones in the house. There is no one in the house but you. Lock your door from the inside. Carefully. Rest in peace.

        Your Host,
        Camilla

The Secret of Laurel Oaks

Lois Ruby

A TOM DOHERTY ASSOCIATES BOOK
NEW YORK

THE SECRET OF LAUREL OAKS

A Starscape Book
Published by Tom Doherty Associates, LLC
175 Fifth Avenue
New York, NY 10010

www.tor-forge.com

ISBN 978-0-7653-5229-3

First Edition: September 2008
First Mass Market Edition: October 2009

Printed in June 2010 in the United States of America by Offset Paperback Manufacturers, Dallas, Pennsylvania.

S   0   9   8   7   6   5   4   3   2   1

For Jacob Chase Ruby

Acknowledgments

Voluminous thanks to the best of writers, readers, and friends: Deb Seely, Dian Curtis Regan, and Clare Vanderpool. Also, thanks to Susan Cohen, an agent with abiding wisdom, and to my husband, Tom Ruby, for his boundless patience. You've all been there with me, even back when Daphne was Chloe.

The Secret of Laurel Oaks

Prologue
Daphne

Listen . . .

That's what you gotta do, listen, and if you've got two ears, well then, you're twice as lucky as I am. Matter of fact, if you're alive, you're a hundred times luckier than me. Can't feel my body twisting in pain anymore, but, same time, I can't feel my heart singing in joy, either, like when *mon cher* Isaac used to come around. Soul-weary, that's what I *can* feel, because I've been watching over this place for most of two centuries, waiting . . . waiting . . .

My name's Daphne. Never did get a second name, but I guess if I had to swear to a name, it'd be Nethercott, after the Judge. Master usually gave his slaves his own family name for a Christian name, but we all just flung that off, like tossing feed to the hogs.

We all had our real names, our African names, the names of our hearts. Tante Drucilla, she said her name was Alaxy, after her Yoruba great-grand, and Eulie's Tom was really Quiamaba, 'cause his daddy's people hailed from a place by the Congo River. I was Dhe, but the Judge's wife gave me Daphne, and I didn't mind.

She was young, Miss Amelia Maye was, still having babies then. Early on, she was a nice lady, too nice for the Judge, if you ask me, the way he carried on. Those days, Miss Amelia treated me like I was people, not like some masters' wives do their slaves. Treat their house hounds better. She taught me how to talk right when I was still in pigtails and shifts. Said, "You're going to be around my babies, my Molly and Alice, and they'll need to hear English spoken in ways pleasing to their discerning ears, even though, bless their souls, they're Louisiana-born. I, myself, was born in Pennsylvania, don't you know. So, heed my words. Listen, and do as I do."

Truth to tell, listening's what got me into big trouble.

I was alive once, long time ago. Nobody knows just what year I was born and baptized Catholic; I think 1824 or '25. *Ma mère*, Henriette, she tried to hide me down in the quarters, told Hector, that wild dog of an overseer, that I died birthing. I s'pose that's the first time I died.

But Hector knew better. Sometimes *Maman* stuffed an old rag or sock in my mouth to keep the crying quiet from Hector. "You ain't *never* gon' be nobody's slave!" she said

over and over. All the *tantes* told me that was my lullaby
first two years. They say my daddy was a coal-skinned
wonder, name of Ventoure. Shoulders broad enough to
carry a felled tree, but I don't know. The Judge sold him
away from us, and Henriette, she just moaned and wailed
for days, even let me cry all I wanted. Then she took the
cholera and died about three, four years later, so the *tantes*
raised me up to about eight years. I was nobody's child,
and everybody's child, switching around from cabin to
cabin.

Miss Amelia stumbled on me when she brought a jar
of clear chicken soup to Tante Drucilla. Tante Drucilla
might have been Henriette's true aunt, or maybe even her
maman. Hard to tell who was whose, those days. Tante
Drucilla was already too old for working the field, so the
Judge retired her, meaning she cooked up big heaping
kettles of cornmeal mush or sweet potato and onion stew
for the whole bunch of us down in the quarters. But that
day when Miss Amelia came with the chicken soup, Tante
Drucilla's stove was cold, because she was down real bad
with the croup.

"Why, which one are you?" Miss Amelia said, putting
the jar on the table so's not to touch Tante Drucilla direct.
"You have such bright eyes."

I'll never forget that. Bright eyes.

"What's your name, child?"

"Dhe, ma'am," I whispered.

"What kind of a proper name is D?" She tapped her
fingernails on Tante Drucilla's teakettle, thinking deep.
Then she pointed at my arm. "Look at you, brown as tree

bark and smooth as an acorn. You look just like the laurel oaks out in front of the Judge's house." Always called her husband *the Judge*, or else *Mr. Nethercott*. "No, D will not do. I believe I'll call you Daphne."

It was three years or more before I found out why she named me that, but Daphne sounded like pure music to me, and the name stuck.

Miss Amelia took me right up to the big house, me waving back to my *tantes* the whole way up the hill. She handed me over to Birdie, who took care of the kitchen and hadn't ever been a field hand like Tante Drucilla. She wasn't a Catholic like the rest of us, neither, 'cause she'd been born over in Alabama.

That's all right. I slept on the floor next to Birdie's stove anyway, and I never had another cold hour until the night my body slapped the wintery waters of the Mississippi. But I was already dead again.

Chapter One

Lila

"Here we are!" Dad said, waking Mom from her short nap. It had been a long Thursday of travel from Albuquerque to Baton Rouge, and after a quick dinner of muffuletta sandwiches at the airport, we had hit the road to get to the bed-and-breakfast before dark.

Though there was room for maybe six cars, the Laurel Oaks parking lot was totally deserted. Where were all the other guests? As our rented SUV crunched the gravel of the plantation grounds, I rolled down my window and stuck my head out. Steamy air blasted my face. It was

October, which in Louisiana means still hot enough to fry bacon on the hood of the car.

The two-story mansion loomed ahead at the end of the driveway, in the dusty shadows of twilight. I couldn't wait to explore the whole place, which was supposed to be one of the ten most haunted houses in the entire country. That is, if you believe the Smithsonian Institution's Web site. "Wow, it really looks—"

"Creepy." My brother Gabe, who's fourteen, a year older than me, had an annoying habit of finishing my sentences, when I was perfectly capable of doing it myself.

We were missing two days of school for our family trek, because Mom had been invited to give a paper at the Biophysical Anthropology Conference at Louisiana State. Since she was always overwhelmed with whatever it is professors do, and Dad was hopelessly nontech, Mom had asked me to hunt down an interesting place to stay.

"And, Lila, make sure it's someplace not at all like Albuquerque," she'd said.

What could be more not like high desert Albuquerque than a swampy plantation? I did an Internet search and came up with a sure winner: "Laurel Oaks is certifiably haunted. Come on, it'll be so much fun!" I'd promised my family back in the summer. Of course, that was before Roberto died and everything changed.

Now my dark spiked hair wilted in the humidity, and my usual gobs of mousse plastered the hair to my forehead. I looked over at Gabe. *His* perfect cap of blond hair bobbed around his face and fell over one eye, making him look like a lopsided cyclops. Even his Balloon Fiesta T-shirt

looked like it'd just come out of the dryer. Me, I was leak-
ing from every pore in the Louisiana soup.

Dad parked the car and we tumbled out. "Ouch!" The
hot gravel burned my bare feet. I leaped to the grass for
relief until Mom tossed me my flip-flops.

Dad looked around, nervously jingling the car keys.
"You got a confirmation, didn't you, Emily?"

"Right here." Mom fanned the yellow paper under his
nose. "It says to park in the back and check in at the General Store. Over there."

"Which has a CLOSED sign on it," Gabe observed.
"They're trying to get under our skin from square one."

"Lila, get the local Comfort Inn on that cell phone
BlackBerry whatever you call it thing of yours."

"No way, Dad!" cried Gabe. "I'm ready to collide head-
on with a bunch of ghouls. You up for it, Lila?"

"Oh, yeah," I murmured, but I had a different take on
it. Ask me a month ago, and I'd have agreed with Gabe
one hundred percent. But at the end of the summer things
changed for me. Because of Roberto. I shuddered at the
thought of his broken body and the weird stuff that came
afterward. Stuff I'd never told *anybody*.

But I trudged right ahead, leading the troops down
the gallery, which was a long porch that spanned the back
of the house. Six rocking chairs lined the gallery, perfectly
still and gleaming white in the dusky moonlight.

The whole house was dark except for one dim bulb
lamp in the window of a second-floor dormer, flickering
the way those fake electric Christmas candles do.

Mom sank into one of the rockers and looked around

wanly. Her Southwest peasant skirt billowed around her like a parachute. "Look at me!" She thrust out an arm puckered with big goose bumps. "I have a bad feeling about this place, kids."

"Lila's idea, her fault," Gabe said gleefully.

Dad glanced my way and smiled. He's absolutely the gentlest of men. "Emily, let's you and I go around to the front. You kids stay put." They walked around the side of the house, holding hands. Embarrassing if anyone else were around to see them.

I rattled every doorknob along the gallery. Each door was locked tight, and each had a horseshoe hanging over it, some good-luck thing. Looked like we were going to *need* a little luck to get inside.

A lamppost over by the courtyard fountain shed thin sprays of light, enough to create a glare against the windows of the house's ground floor. Peering in, I saw that it was filled with dark furniture as massive as bears, and huge hanging chandeliers, and shimmery mirrors and unlit sconces, and the faint outline of a back staircase, but no people.

"There's got to be an innkeeper around," Gabe said. "Or a caretaker, or janitor or someone."

We cupped our hands against the window glare and peered into the back side of the reception hall. A dim lamp suddenly sputtered on. I jumped.

"Motion detector," Gabe said.

"Yeah, but whose motion?" Nobody stirred inside. The old-fashioned lamp revealed a baby-grand piano with its top raised like the wing of a swooping eagle. A pot of yellow mums perched on the piano, centered on a lace doily.

I grabbed Gabe's arm. "Look!"

The piano keys were rising and falling rapidly, all the way up and down the keyboard, as though someone were playing a jaunty tune.

Gabe put his sweaty ear to the window. "Hear anything?"

Not a sound came from the room, and the piano bench was empty.

"It's a player piano with the sound gutted out," Gabe said. "Pretty convincing."

"Probably. Sure." I watched those silent keys jump up and down as though ghostly fingers tapped them. And then the flowerpot began inching toward the end of the piano as the lace doily seemed to be pulled slowly out from under it. I gasped.

Gabe just snorted. "Look for wires," he said. "Somebody's behind a chair, jerking that pot across the piano. I'll bet money on it."

"What money? You owe me five dollars already," I muttered, heart pounding as the pot hung off the edge of the piano for a second until gravity kicked in, and the mums came crashing to the floor. More dirt than could possibly have filled that small pot scattered all over the threadbare Persian rug.

"Whoa!" I cried.

"Just special effects to spook gullible people like you," Gabe scoffed.

By now gray dusk had slid into navy-blue night. Gabe

trotted along the porch, and as he whooshed by, he set all six rockers in furious motion, their legs slamming against the ancient floorboards. A minute passed, then another.

"Weird," I said, trying to sound unconcerned. "There's no wind to keep the rockers going."

"Electromagnetic something or other," Gabe said.

I swirled my hand around the middle chair, as if I could grab a fistful of ghost or charged air. Nothing. A shiver went down my back. I glanced over at our SUV. Maybe we could still get a room somewhere else. Anywhere else. The fierce churning song of cicadas filled the night. "This place creeps me out."

"That's the beauty of it," Gabe replied. And the chairs kept thumping.

"What's that racket?" asked Dad as he and Mom came around to the back of the house.

"The old lady ghosts are racing to the edge of the veranda in their rocking chairs," Gabe replied dryly.

"So I see." Dad tossed the car keys from hand to hand. "I guess it's no surprise that every single door's locked all around the house."

"I don't like this place, Ethan. The management must have forgotten that we were checking in tonight." Mom rolled her long, salt-and-pepper hair into a knot that she tucked in at the top of her head. Rivers of sweat streamed down her face and neck. My mom, who'd done fieldwork in remote rain forest villages of South America where natives speared poisonous snakes for lunch, looked positively spooked by Laurel Oaks.

"Just one night," Dad reassured her, and she grudgingly nodded.

Gabe strode along the porch, his sneakers slapping the splintery wood. This time as he passed, every rocker stopped suddenly, some tilting back on their legs in freeze-frame.

"How'd they do *that*?" I yelped.

"Good trick, and here's our next clue." A banana tree loomed in the corner between the General Store and the house. Gabe pulled an envelope out of its tangle of floppy huge leaves. "Must have been blown over here by the wind."

What wind? The air was unnaturally still, as if the night held us all in suspension, and not even a leaf dared to flutter. And yet, without a breath of cool air, I felt chills ripple up and down my back. I huddled close to Gabe. He waved the envelope. Printed on the front were these words:

The Barry Party

Us. That made me think of the Donner Party in the 1840s, a bunch of people in covered wagons trekking from Illinois to California to pan for gold. They got stranded in the wintery mountains, ran out of food, and then it was down to feast on friends and family or starve. Too bad Gabe was too skinny and sinewy to provide much tender meat for the Barry party.

An old-fashioned skeleton key, glinting gold, tumbled out of the envelope and clattered to the floor. I swooped it up while Gabe tilted a sheet of onionskin paper toward the lamplight and read aloud:

Welcome to Laurel Oaks Plantation.
I'm frightfully glad you're here.

- *Do not attempt to enter the General Cambridge Suite at the far end of the gallery.*
- *The golden key opens the door at the bottom of the steep staircase leading to the dark belly of the house.*
  BEWARE THE TWELFTH STEP.
- *Keys wait in the doors of your rooms at the top of the stairs. The Eberly room is on your right; the Brookes and Gladstone rooms are on your left. Choose wisely.*
- *Caution:* **Do not, DO NOT** *turn out the* **light in the hall.** *When the last light at Laurel Oaks is snuffed out, the spirits are released to take their pleasure.*
- *There are no phones in the house. There is no one in the house but you. Lock your door from the inside. Carefully. Rest in peace.*

Your Host,
Camilla

"They certainly know how to set atmosphere around here." Dad laughed out loud as he folded the welcome note into his shirt pocket.

"No kidding," Gabe said. "Rest in peace, that's what they say when you're six feet under, eating worms!"

Dad, Gabe, and even Mom were all laughing, while my heart raced and my curiosity went into overdrive.

Of course, the thing I most wanted to know was, what's in the General Cambridge Suite?

Chapter Two
Daphne

Used to be called the Cambridge Plantation, named for Miss Amelia's daddy when he came down here after bad business up north, something about rum or whiskey, one.

The Cambridges, they brought along Luke Mullin to tend their kitchen garden. Like his daddy, and *his* daddy before him, Luke Mullin was a free black man, only one I ever knew. I s'pose he could of gone up north and worked for money, but our folks whispered around that Luke Mullin was *fou* in the head or else too shy or scared to go off on his own, even with free papers. So, he lived in a shed way apart from the rest of us, because we weren't none of us free.

He could make anything grow, could make flowers spring from old cork. The fields are overgrown with wild bushes, now. Gotta wonder if Eulie's spirit got caught in the thicket somewhere around the place. I bet being dead hasn't improved her none. If I ever saw her nowadays, I'd stay clear of that girl. Even back then, none of us had any use for her stirring up the pot, not even Luke Mullin, the mildest of souls.

Old cross-eyed Luke, he never could look me in the eye or talk to me direct. He's long gone now. No planting's been done here for more than a hundred years—not indigo, not cotton, not even the house greens that Luke Mullin used to grow for the supper table, or those flowers that did us in. Back then, Luke plugged a couple dozen laurel saplings in the ground, and that's why the name of this place got changed. Laurel Oaks Plantation. They're all gone now, those laurels.

My own tree's a big old live oak. Anybody could look at him in the light of day and know he's Daphne's tree. He used to listen to me, like he had ears his own self, and he talked to me, too, even told me his name. Timberlarken. True. I couldn't of made up a name like that. I believe he's been around since the beginning, since the Garden of Eden, and he'll still be here at the great reckoning, come the end of days when *tous les saints* go marching home. He'll still be holding all my secrets and rememories in his wavy leaves. But I don't go to my tree anymore. Scares me too much.

Lots of folks stay at our place time to time, ghost-hunters mostly wanting to prove we're real, or else wanting to prove we're not. Sweet Jesus must be having a laugh over that!

Most of those folks don't have it in them to see us, at least not the way we want to be seen. When Birdie was alive, she used to say, "Some folks just ain't got the third eye to see with." She must have had a hundred eyes, 'cause my Birdie saw into everybody as clear as glass. She's not around this place anymore, neither. She finished up what the Lord sent her here to do, and I 'spect she's having a good long rest on a featherbed up there in heaven.

These folks came tonight right before dark. They look like a nice family with a loving *maman* and daddy, a sister and brother who don't snarl at each other too bad. Now, that boy, seems like his feet came from somebody else. They're too big for his body, but what do I know about boys?

I do know girls. That one they call Lila, something about her stirs my soul. Her hair stands up straight off her head all spiny. Reminds me a lot of Miss Amelia's youngest, Molly, who never did want me messing with her hair that was a bird's nest if you didn't watch it. My Molly was always a breath away from trouble half the day, like this Lila, I 'spect, but she's scared of something, too. Don't know what, yet. Couple times I passed right in front of her, see if she'd notice. She did, just didn't know *what* she noticed. I believe she has the third eye. Got to watch myself, filling up with hope. I've been fooled before.

A dark-skinned girl's been living here a while with the fool Camilla who's always touring folks around the place. Sal's the girl's name. She sits down at the piano now and then and pounds out a few notes, but not like my Alice, bless her heart. Miss Amelia's oldest, she used to play the piano like a dream, with her lily-white hands arched so dainty, and just the pads of her fingers racing over the keys so pretty, you hardly noticed a sour note. She still plays, like tonight, sorrowful and sweet.

Sal's younger than I was when I was alive. Wait 'til she meets that Lila girl. Seems to me those two might be birds of a feather.

Not like Alice and Molly, who were as different as a banana to a watermelon. Molly couldn't sit still on the piano bench for more than a blink without falling off or knocking over the flowerpot, or slamming down that big heavy lid. The child, bless her soul, could find mischief worse than anybody I ever saw. One time she jumped in the trough where we watered the pigs, then rolled around in the dirt until her dress was gray as rain clouds. Miss Amelia had a fit, because she wanted her girls done up like ladies every minute. "Molly Cambridge Nethercott, get that dress off this instant!" Miss Amelia said, and I knew what was coming next. "Daphne, scrub this dress over the washboard as long as it takes to get it white again. This is a disgrace!"

Back in my time when they called the big house Cambridge House, Birdie was queen of the kitchen, and I was her go-get-it girl, happy as a meadowlark. Ooh, what didn't I learn from Birdie! She spun all kinds of *voudoun* spells. Hoodoo, we called it. Like, take a shank of red flannel and sew up a gris-gris bag. Stuff it full with nail clippings, ground-up frog bone, red sneezing pepper. Sprinkle on a pinch of goofer dust from the graveyard out beyond and give it to somebody to make him lovesick. Turn his heart, just like that. The right magic, you can make him weak as a baby chick, or sick to his innards, or crazy in the head. Make him dumb 'til his tongue just rolls around in his mouth like a tough clot of *mouton*. Then you turn right around and make him whole, again. Birdie was a conjure woman, all right. Wasn't anything Birdie couldn't do.

Two, three years after me and Birdie sweated side by side in the kitchen, I got to stringing chestnuts with her boy, Isaac. You did that, strung chestnuts and hung 'em around your neck when you liked a boy. Isaac, he paraded by the kitchen window every chance he got to catch sight of me. Once he stuck a bunch of white flowers in Birdie's peach pie cooling on the windowsill. When Birdie saw that, she just grinned, showing big dark spaces. Real teasing-like, she said, "Take care those posies ain't no 'lander."

Everybody *knows* oleander's about the prettiest thing out there, but it's poison—roots, bark, sap, and even those buttery-colored flowers. Pure poison, I tell you.

Chapter Three

Lila

Gabe laughed at the mysterious welcome note. "Talk about hokey, this is a cheap version of the haunted mansion at Disneyland. What a ride we're gonna have."

"This is absurd," Mom said, slapping the note. "Tonight I've got to get inside and read over my presentation for the conference, but tomorrow night we're staying at a normal hotel."

"Feeling a little squeamish, Emily?"

"Not at all," Mom huffed.

"You look gorgeous in the lamplight, my dear." Dad—what a hopeless romantic.

"Yeah, if you like greenish vampire skin," Gabe said.

A glance at Mom in the ghoulish light made *me* a little squeamish. She seemed almost transparent. I heard a faint voice in my ear, or in the wind, or in the rustling of leaves. I shook my head to chase the voice away and shaded my eyes to look in the window of the reception hall again. I was sure I'd see someone in there pulling the strings. Things do not move on their own, just as voices don't come on the wind.

I jumped—the mum plant now sat cheerfully in the center of the lace doily again. Magic? No. Somebody was definitely in the house.

"Great prop!" Gabe said as a black cat padded up to the porch. It swished its tail across my bare legs.

"Yeow!" I leaped, setting the rockers in motion again. The mangy thing turned its head and glared at me, with eyes flecked and gleaming yellow as aggie marbles, knowing eyes, then sauntered away from us and began scratching at the door at the end of the gallery. The General Cambridge Suite. The one we were told to stay away from. The door loomed ahead, and the cat sat down in front of it, looking smugly over her shoulder at us.

Gabe moved toward the cat. "Here, kitty-kitty, you miserable feline!"

"Don't go over there," I warned Gabe.

"Right. It's probably booby-trapped, and the cat's leading us smack into the snare."

"You're certainly giving that animal more credit than it's due," Dad said. "Let's go inside. Maybe it's cooler in there."

I handed him the key, which he tried. It didn't seem to fit the hole.

"Swell. We'll be sleeping in the hyperactive rockers," Gabe said, tapping his foot.

"Here, Ethan, let me." Mom took the key out of Dad's hand and tried jamming it into the lock. Then she turned the key upside down, and it slid in smoothly. We piled inside. "Slam the door quick, don't let the cat in." Mom had always been afraid of cats.

The back entryway was shadowy-dark, with just the black wing of the piano visible in the next room. I couldn't see if the keys were playing or not, but there wasn't a sound coming from the parlor except the steady tick-tock of a clock. Brown and white nubby wallpaper covered the east wall, with a murky mirror smack in the center. Gabe mugged in front of the mirror, but I didn't want to look. Lately it had spooked me to see my face in the mirror of a darkened room.

Suddenly the unseen clock went *BONG!!* which sent me flying into Dad's arms.

"There, there," he said, patting me gently. "We're all a bit jittery. A good night's sleep and some fine Loosiana crawfish étouffée tomorrow will have us all feeling more like ourselves." Dad's a food writer and one of those people who think that food solves all problems. He added, "Let's go up to our rooms and settle in, shall we?"

I sniffed the air. "Anybody smell candle wax?"

"I smell mold," Gabe said, leading the way to the stairs.

He marched up the first carpeted steps of the dark stairway, with his trombone case and a duffel of his baseball gear in front of him. He always came prepared, in case a pickup game suddenly required the talents of the future White Sox shortstop. The rest of us trailed him, dragging our bags.

I counted the steps. "Nine, ten, eleven." *Beware the twelfth step.* "Watch out, Gabe, the next one's the step they warned us about."

"Ooooh," Gabe teased as he leaped over it.

I carefully placed my foot on the twelfth step, held my breath, then sort of ground my heel into it. Nothing happened. Was I disappointed—or relieved?

"Keep going," Mom urged behind me.

Upstairs, we unlocked the three rooms offered us in the welcome note. Gabe took the Gladstone room. As his door clunked against the wall, he bellowed, "Vamoose, you spirits. We're here to take possession."

Mom sank into the maroon velvet chaise longue in the Brookes Room and hung her feet over its arm. "This will do us nicely, Ethan, don't you think? You'll be right across the hall in the Maude Eberly room, Lila, so we're all cozy close," she said, unzipping her laptop case.

Dad pulled Mom's strictly business suit out of their bag and hung it in the gigantic dark brown wardrobe. "Your mother still has work to do this evening, Lila, so let's call it a night."

"It's a night," I said.

"I can always count on you for that one." Dad gave me his sweet buck-toothed smile. "Remind your brother to set his alarm for seven-thirty sharp. You, too, so we can have a hearty lumberjack's breakfast in town and be on our way to the university by nine-thirty."

Mom propped her laptop up on her stomach. "Goodnight kiss?" she said vaguely. Gabe and I were convinced she was the original absentminded professor, lost in her mysterious head work. I dropped a kiss on her cheek, hugged Dad, and backed out of the room.

The Maude Eberly room looked so Southern-comfort with the mosquito netting draped over a bed high enough that I'd need a stool to climb up to it. I flashed on the light. An ancient vanity covered in a lace doily hunkered against one wall, with a swinging mirror above it. In the corner stood a coat rack with limbs like antlers, and perched on one of the horns was a peacock feather hat with a long pearl-tipped hat pin sticking out of it. When Gabe saw it, he'd say something smart-mouthed, like *you could do surgery with a thing like this. Watch your tonsils.*

I left the door open, which I never did at home. Mom and Dad's door was already closed, and I heard the shower running. *They* had a private bathroom; Gabe and I'd have to share the one in the hall.

Across the hall, Gabe's baseball bat clunked onto the hardwood floor. In a minute he yelled, "Lila! Come here, look at this thing on the wall."

I padded across the cool hardwood floor to see what he was talking about.

"See? Read it. My guy's Samuel Gladstone, the one who croaked on the stairs. Poor Sammy-boy, dead as roadkill right there on the twelfth step."

Then I wondered who Maude Eberly was. Maybe something on my wall explained it. Heading back to my room, I noticed the lamp on the window seat in the hall. "Gabe? Check out this lamp." He ventured out of his room. "Think it's the light we saw flickering from outside?"

"Yeah, the one that's never supposed to go out, or the spirits roam free. Woo-woo!" Gabe waved his fingers in front of my eyes and sang me the old *Twilight Zone* ditty. "You heard it here first, folks: before the night's over, the master puppeteers will snuff that light out."

Just then a cat leaped onto the table, knocking the lamp on its side and pushing the red shade up at a sick angle. I jumped a foot!

Gabe said, "Hey, didn't Dad make sure the door was closed so the cat couldn't get in?"

"Must be another cat." But I knew it wasn't. Those same glinty yellow eyes stared at us, as if to say, *What are you doing here?*

I carefully reached out to stand the lamp up. The cat hissed at me. A paw shot out and scratched a thin streak down my arm. "Ow!" I jerked my arm back. "Hope the beast doesn't have rabies."

"Beast? She's just a seven-pound kitten." Gabe lunged for the cat, grabbed it around its belly, and ran down the stairs, with the cat mewling all the way.

"Be careful of the twelfth step," I yelled, just in case.

The shower had gone off in Mom and Dad's room, and now I heard her laptop set to the classical music that thrilled them and usually put me right to sleep. The muffled voices were probably Mom reading her speech aloud to Dad, and Dad making a few gentle recommendations—which Mom would ignore.

The downstairs door slammed. Gabe galloped back up the stairs. "Cat's gone. I strangled her and tossed her carcass into the woods."

"Gabriel!"

"Just kidding. She's outside digging up a mouse for dinner."

"You sure she's out?" For some reason, an uneasy feeling deep in the pit of my stomach told me this: no matter how many times we put the cat out, she'd return and those sickly yellow eyes would peer at me from every dark corner of the house.

The cat *owned* the house and I'd swear she wanted us out of it.

Chapter Four
Daphne

Isaac stopped coming by so much when the Judge took a fancy to me. Just the smell of that perfumey mess the Judge splashed on his neck made my stomach churn. I smelled him coming down the stairs about every night and wanted to run for the henhouse, but he'd of found me, and done me worse than he usually did.

I think Miss Amelia knew what was going on under her own roof. The looks she gave me when I brought out her morning soft-cooked eggs and chicory coffee, they cut like knives. Blamed *me*, when it was her man come paying me hateful visits too many nights to count. Only good thing about the Judge is that he made sure all of us got shoes when winter came on, and he was real good about giving us clean wood for coffins when one of our folks passed over.

Judge said I should feel honored. Said he could of gone after any girl around the place, and he picked me special. Wished he'd of given the *honor* to Eulie. The two of them deserved each other. One day Miss Amelia called Eulie up to the house, talked to her on the back porch. She sure couldn't take Eulie into the parlor, all basted with field sweat like she was. Miss Amelia said, "Eulie, you get on well with Birdie, do you not?"

"Yes'm."

I watched and listened out the open window while Alice played the piano and Molly tried to shove her behind right off the piano bench.

"Well, Eulie, I'm thinking of bringing you up here to help out in the kitchen. Birdie could certainly use a hand."

"Daphne?" That one word coming off Eulie's lips sent a chill up my spine.

"I have other plans for Daphne," Miss Amelia said.

"I be up here soon's you call me, Miss Amelia," Eulie said. Ooh, and I knew her, knew the pure joy in her voice, thinking she'd take my place.

Now, Eulie had some dark hoodoo to her. Mean to the core, like a rotted apple. I believe she was a *sorcière*, one of those witches that climbs out of her skin time to time and squeezes into the skin of a cat, and rides people 'til they wake up weary and sore like they've been picking cotton all night instead of resting their bones. I could never prove it about Eulie, but I sure suspicioned it.

The parlor door was open that morning when Miss Amelia and the Judge talked about Eulie and me, like us working in the house had no ears or minds to hear them, or we weren't even there except for our hands and feet to fetch and run after what they needed. See, I had lots of practice being invisible, which comes in handy nowadays.

Heard Miss Amelia say, "As much as you love Birdie's gumbo, Mr. Nethercott, and her peach dumplings and sweet potato pie, the old girl's not going to live forever. Forty, fifty years is about the best we can get from these Negroes, and I believe Birdie's way up near fifty."

"You thinking of retiring her, my dear?" Seemed like he wasn't too interested in the conversation. I heard him rattling that newspaper he read every morning.

Miss Amelia set her tinkly teacup down in the saucer. Those blue-and-white plates were about as thin as her papery skin. Hold them up to the window, and you could see the light right through them. Said, "I've spoken to Eulie. She seems bright enough. She can learn Birdie's recipes. And as for Daphne, she won't be needed around here after a while."

The corners of my jaw tightened like someone'd turned screws in them.

Alice heard her mother say that about me. She stopped the piano and turned the saddest eyes toward me. I scooted Molly down the bench and sat between the two girls, one arm around each of them, dark skin over white dresses, pretty as you please. In a minute the girls got the itch to go outside. My Alice said, "Come on, Molly, let's go see if the hens have been busy." Molly ran to fetch the egg basket and Alice whispered to me, "Mama's gonna send you down, I just know it."

When they were both gone, I moved closer to the parlor, put my ear to the door. Didn't want to miss a single word because they were talking about sending me down to the quarters, about putting me out to the fields, picking the cotton out in the mean sun. Slow death, that way. See how old Eulie looked, how dusty and baggy the skin that held her bones together? And she barely ten years more than me, twenty-five years old, at most, and dark as a barrel of molasses. That's what the fields will do to you.

I worried a piece of string in my apron pocket while they talked and I guess I got a mite careless, because I didn't hear the Judge rear up. When he opened the door, there I was, plain as a hairy wart on your nose. The Judge caught me listening, all right. Well, shoot, I listened to my master and missus 'bout all my life, that's true. *Daphne, fetch me a glass of brandy. Daphne, mind that little one, see she doesn't get into the coal bin. Daphne, a chill's come over me. Stoke up that fire right quick, and hand me my lap robe.* I listened, and I did what I was told, mostly.

That one day, I guess the Judge was feeling just a touch guilty about leaving his wife's bed for my pallet behind the stove most nights, and then fixing to toss me out of the house, just like the Lord tossed Adam and Eve out of that Eden paradise place. And you know how it goes. You feel bad about something and you turn right around and lay the blame on somebody else. So, the Judge had it in for me that day.

"You'll pay for this infernal eavesdropping," he swore, calm as anything, and then I knew I was in for it, all right.

Hurt a whole lot when Hector, the overseer, struck off my ear in one clean slice, like he was splitting a log. I screeched like a shot-up possum, blood spurting all over and sopping up my dress. Never *did* wash all that blood out, and Birdie just tore up the ruined thing for mop rags. I'd of been glad to die that day, hurting so, but I didn't. Lived to see worse.

Oh, I am bone-weary down to my soul. I'm needing something, someone to put me at peace. Don't know what, don't know who, but I'm waiting . . . waiting . . . for somebody.

Could be that Lila with the spiny hair. But she's gonna have a passel of work around here to set things right. Maybe she's got the magic to send me home for good. Maybe Birdie's saving me a featherbed up the way from her, for me and *mon cher* Isaac together. Do hope so.

Chapter Five

Lila

Alone in the Maude Eberly Room that first night, I
stuffed my T-shirts and underwear in the antique dresser.
Every sound echoed in the room—the drawer slamming,
the swing mirror squeaking, my footsteps on the hardwood floor. I wondered what I'd hear in the middle of the
night, huddled under that mosquito netting. The same
thing I'd been hearing at home in the dead of night? Roberto chanting in his native language? The faint, distant
drums?

Roberto Aragon was a Jemez Indian in the program
Mom ran at UNM for Native Americans and Spanish

speakers. He was special, what Mom calls a nontraditional student, meaning he was in college way late. He already had a wife, two kids, and a granddaughter that he was struggling to support as a roofer. The whole Aragon family hung around our house a lot. Sometimes Gabe and I babysat the new baby, Lupita, who kicked and kicked when I changed her diaper like she was already practicing to dance.

Every Christmas, when all the pueblos danced, our family spent the day at Jemez. The dancers wore fur and leather, with some in huge antlers or eagle feathers, and they danced for hours until I thought they'd drop. We weren't supposed to ask questions or take pictures. It's not like they were dancing just to entertain people who had a few hours to kill on Christmas. These were religious dances and chants with secret, sacred meanings—not ours to know.

My feet would tap the pinkish sand of the plaza, and I'd sway to the repetitious chanting of the drummer men, nearly hypnotized. When the dancers broke midday, we'd be swept up in the crowd heading for their cars, except we'd turn into the heart of the pueblo for lunch with Roberto's family.

That night at Laurel Oaks, I wondered what would happen come Christmas. Would we still go to Jemez, even though Roberto was dead? I thought about the low, flat roofs of the pueblo and how strange it was that Roberto picked roofing as a job. He'd been working way up in the clear sky of Albuquerque on a ten-story office building on Candelaria. He slipped on a ceramic shingle and tumbled

down. Landed in the bed of his truck loaded with the rest
of the tiles, which shattered with the force of his body.

We weren't allowed inside the pueblo cemetery, but
Mom, Dad, Gabe, and I were the only Anglos just beyond its
fence when Roberto was laid to rest. Since then, I'd heard his
chanting, his drumming, on three moonless nights. I think.
What else could it be? Of course, I didn't tell anyone. Even
my own family would think I was a lunatic, and maybe I
was, hearing ghostly sounds that way.

At least there at Laurel Oaks, *famous* for its ghosts, I
could absolutely prove that no such thing existed. Roberto's spirit couldn't follow me a thousand miles, could it?

I slammed the drawer shut and heard a light tapping
on the door. "Come on in, Gabe." Tapping again, not Gabe's
usual, which was pound twice and stomp right in. "If you're
just trying to spook me," I shouted through the door,
"you've failed miserably." I threw the door open—and there
stood a woman holding a thick yellow candle.

"Welcome, I am Camilla, the caretaker of this house.
The candlelight tour begins at nine." Her voice was scratchy
and very Southern. She had mocha-shaded skin, an old-
fashioned calico dress that brushed the ankles of her
pointy hightop boots, and black hair done up in some
complicated bird's nest woven with feathers and twigs.

"But . . . but your note said we were the only ones in
the house," I stammered.

"Except me," she said, holding that candle in both hands
like a bridesmaid bouquet.

"And me." A small girl peeked around the billowy
dress. Camilla tried to stuff her back, but the girl stepped

out into the dim light of the hall in a dress the miniature of the woman's. She was about nine, or a very small ten, with skin ten shades darker than Camilla's, and hair trimmed to little more than fuzz around her head. She gazed at me with huge eyes, lots of white surrounding dark buttons. "You're Lila, right?"

Surprised, I asked, "How do you know my name?"

"I heard your brother and them call you."

"Sal, hush now," Camilla said, then to me, "Just as the clock strikes nine, y'all had best assemble in the reception hall below for the tour."

"I'll get my brother, but our parents have gone to bed. They'll pass."

Camilla and Sal exchanged a look. "*Pass* is what we say when someone leaves this world and moves on to the next," Camilla said.

Freaky. "I just meant they wouldn't be on the tour."

"Their unfortunate choice," Camilla said somberly. "Without the candlelight tour, the Laurel Oaks experience is shallow." Starting down the stairs, Sal trailing her, she paused at the twelfth and turned to shoot me a stage whisper over her shoulder, "Exactly when the clock strikes nine," she warned, and sank lower and lower until only the tip of her candle flame was visible.

The grandfather clock downstairs began to bong. One . . . two. I pounded on the Samuel Gladstone door. "Showtime, Gabe! Come on, I'll explain on the way down, but we've got to hurry." Three . . . four . . . five.

We thundered down the stairs. Two black wrought-iron sconces flanking a big, fancy mirror provided the only light in the front reception hall, except for Camilla's candle that shot shadows around the room and left corners eerily dark.

Just at the ninth resounding bong, Camilla began her patter. "Welcome to Laurel Oaks." (As if we hadn't already met.) "This remarkable house was built in 1794 on Tunica Indian burial grounds."

"They shoulda known better." This from Sal, in my ear.

I whispered a quick intro: "Sal—my brother, Gabe."

Camilla cleared her throat impatiently. "Look over here to my right." She whipped the candle around to the mirror, black smoke trailing. The flame of the candle flickered back, doubled now in the reflection. "Gaze at the mirror with your inner eye."

I stiffled a giggle, because she sounded like a corny fortune-teller.

"Back then, when there came a death in the house—and don't think there weren't at least a dozen mysterious deaths here, suicides, murders, you name it. So, whenever someone *passed*, folks covered every painting and looking glass to keep out the evil spirits. But one time a careless maid forgot to cover this one mirror in front of y'all and, well, see the results for yourselves."

Gabe and I inched forward. It just looked like a plain old smudgy mirror.

"Look close. Lots of folks see a face in the mirror, and the outline of Daphne's turban. Others see dripping blood."

"Who's Daphne?" Gabe asked.

"It'll be revealed to y'all in the fullness of time," Camilla replied in her fake spooky rasp.

Wait. I *could* sort of see a black splotch that seemed to drip down the murky glass. And the faint outline of a face. Did Gabe see it?

"Needs a blast of Windex," he said.

"Ah, a cynic! But let me tell y'all, the glass has been replaced at least nine times in the last 170 years, am I right, Sal, nine times?"

"Yes, ma'am," Sal droned, without much enthusiasm.

Gabe whispered to me, "They probably do this act every night, and poor Sal's bored to death with it."

"Shh! I don't think you're supposed to say *to death* in a ghost house." I surpressed a smile and elbowed Gabe to pay attention as Camilla continued.

"And each time, *each time,* the dark image reappears. Why? Y'all will have to decide for yourselves."

She led us to the fancy dining room, just about dwarfed by a crystal chandelier. The long table was set for dinner with silverware thick enough to drive nails into concrete. An army of stiff-backed chairs surrounded the fortress of the table. It looked like a very stuffy party was about to start—two centuries ago.

"For years this room was off-limits until the Brookes bought the house from the Nethercotts. This is the very room where the little Nethercott girls ate the fateful, tainted birthday cake."

"You telling us they were poisoned?" Gabe asked.

Camilla beamed at him. "For a fact! Daphne, of course, is the one who crumbled the poisonous oleander leaves into the cake, thinking she'd make the girls a little bit sick, and then she'd nurse them back to health and win the favor of the Judge and Mrs. Nethercott, her master and mistress."

"So she was a slave?" Gabe asked

"What else would she be, a Negro girl of fifteen in 1839 Louisiana?" Camilla replied.

"You don't hear nobody saying 'Negro' no more," Sal said, snickering, and Camilla glared at her. "Oops, done it again! Sorry, ma'am."

"Then what happened?" I asked.

"Ah, yes, the tragedy of Laurel Oaks. Daphne's scheme backfired, and the girls *and* their mother, Amelia Raye Cambridge Nethercott, all went to meet their Maker that night."

Chapter Six

Lila

Sure, reading about Laurel Oaks on the Internet had been cool, but being there in the very house sent prickles through me, leaving me chilled, like when a cloud blocks out the sun. It's all just a myth, I told myself, meanwhile searching dark corners. But was it possible that three people had actually been poisoned right there in that room?

Camilla continued, "Well, so, after that wretched night, poor bereaved Judge Nethercott sealed this room off. Y'all can just imagine his abiding sorrow, losing his wife and both daughters in one fell swoop."

"What happened to Daphne?" I demanded.

Camilla seemed startled by my tone. "Why, she's one of our resident ghosts, isn't she, Sal?"

Sal tugged at my T-shirt. I turned around, and she nodded, like she really believed Daphne was a resident ghost. Gabe saw it, too, and shrugged in a *beats-me* gesture.

"Now, let's move along, shall we?" Next Camilla showed us the button in the newel post that let visitors in the 1830s know that the mortgage was paid off, and drapes hanging in folds on the floor, like somebody'd made a mistake measuring. "Ah, y'all have noticed the yards of wasted fabric. That's the way folks used to show how rich they were."

I tuned her out. Who cared about drapes? I wondered about Daphne. A fifteen-year-old girl, a girl close to my age, poisoning three people? Did she mean to kill them? Was it a terrible accident? Maybe she didn't do it.

A shadow on the floor caught my eye. I squinted, trying to see it better in the faint light.

It was an odd shape, almost like. . . . Suddenly I stopped dead, slamming into Gabe.

"Hey, watch it!" he snapped.

"What's that on the floor!" I pointed to a muzzy image.

Camilla jerked her head around. "That? By the door?" I nodded. Camilla squared her shoulders indignantly. "You've taken this tour before. I might have guessed, the way you two were carrying on."

"No, I haven't, I swear." The image was fading, and I felt the color slowly returning to my face. It must have been a trick of the light. I looked up, trying to spot a hidden projector. Or it was just my imagination. Now it was gone.

Camilla played the scene for every drop of juice she could squeeze out of it. With the pointed toe of her boot, she drew the familiar shape on the floor, like on a cop show. "Just about the size of a man's body," she said, her eyes glowing in the eerie candlelight. "A long time ago, a soldier died in this very spot. Some people can see him down to his tattered uniform and his scuffed boots."

I saw it again, in my mind, like a reflection in water, then just a vague outline shimmering, and gone.

"Now, watch what happens," Camilla said. "Sal, honey?"

The girl pointed a stockinged foot toward the spot where I'd seen—or not seen—the body. She jammed that foot forward until it seemed to hit an invisible barrier, then she jumped back, rubbing the stubbed toes. " 'Bout down to three toes, now."

Camilla flashed her a look, then continued, "Many of our housekeepers have reported not being able to force their mops into this area. Most people have no problem stepping into this space, though. Go ahead, y'all step foot here."

Gabe hopscotched right about where the dead soldier's heart would be, skipping into the space on one foot and then out.

"Let me try." I kicked my foot forward, but it seemed to thunk a wall. Camilla smiled, probably assuming I was faking just like Sal, but the truth is, I simply could *not* force my foot onto that spot. And then it went through the wall to something squishy. I yanked my foot back fast, letting out a cry.

"What's the deal, Lila?" asked Gabe.

Sal's eyes grew wide as she stared up at me. That's when I realized that Sal hadn't been faking at all, and I *had* seen the body!

Gabe wrapped his arm around my shoulders. "You okay?"

I nodded, not at all sure I was.

Camilla eyed us suspiciously, then led us past the parlor with the piano that we'd seen from the back porch, with the flowerpot right in place. At the end of the porch was the room we'd been warned not to enter.

My voice trembled a little as I asked, "Camilla, I'm wondering what's in the General Cambridge Suite."

"Oh, no doubt y'all are all wondering." She licked her lips, and I thought that meant she was ready to give us a long story, but instead she said, "I'm not at liberty to say just now. Maybe in a week or so."

"But we won't be here next week!" I protested.

"What a pity." She led us to the staircase. "Follow me upstairs, please." Camilla bunched up her skirt and ceremoniously counted each step, with Sal right behind her. On the twelfth step, they stopped and turned toward us, while Gabe and I hunched against the banister.

I looked down the stairs to the soldier's body by the front door. Nothing there. There never was, I told myself over and over, and yet my foot knew better.

"Hey, Camilla, I've got another question for you," Gabe said. "Where's the cat door?"

"Cat door?" she asked, as if this were a weird question, in a place where *everything* was totally off the wall.

"Yeah, one of those little holes with a flap that a cat uses to get in and out," Gabe explained.

Camilla huffed, "No such thing in this house. Oh, mercy, has that scruffy cat been slinking around here again? Sal, have you been sneaking a bowl of milk out to her?"

"No, ma'am. She just comes by if we feed her or don't."

"Next time I spot her, I'll—never mind. Now, let's talk about Samuel Gladstone, who was a son-in-law of the Brookes family. This would have been just after the War."

"She means the Civil War," Gabe explained to me. "Only one that counts down here."

"Yankees, I suspected as much," Camilla said with a snort.

"Not Yankees. We're from Albuquerque, New Mexico," Gabe told her.

"Ah, the great Southwest." Camilla sneered. "Well, here in Louisiana we call it the War of Northern Aggression. Nothing civil about it, though Mr. Lincoln did a good thing or two after a long while. So, as I was telling y'all, one night, in the middle of a dinner party, Mr. Samuel Gladstone was called to the front porch by an insistent bellpull going on and on."

"Here it comes!" Sal warned. She clapped her hands over her ears as Camilla reached for a button on the wall that released an awful screechy sound like a bicycle bell desperate for oil.

"A little unsettling, is it?" Camilla said. "Now, listen here. Samuel Gladstone got up from the table to answer that infernal bell, and there stood some unidentified man who'd come on horseback. Before Mr. Gladstone knew what hit him, that merciless stranger shot the poor man dead."

Gabe said, "A gallop-by shooting."

Sal snickered, and Camilla gave her a withering look. "Sorry, ma'am," Sal murmured. "Don't know what gets into me, sometimes."

"Yes. Well, the story doesn't end there. You see, Mr. Gladstone stumbled into the house and struggled up these stairs and died right here, right *here*, on this very step." She stomped her foot for emphasis.

"Died in the arms of his wife," Sal added.

"Did I not say that?"

"No, ma'am, but you usually do."

"Hmmn. So, to this day people hear Samuel Gladstone's footsteps thumping all the way up to this stair." She panned us with the candle. "Shh. You hear anything?"

Just the sputtering of the candle. We followed her up the rest of the stairs. She unlocked one of the guest rooms to let us peek in. "This is where the youngest little girl slept her final night on earth."

Chilling. I was glad I hadn't gotten that room. So I asked, "What can you tell us about the Maude Eberly Room, where I'm staying?"

"There is truly a story associated with that chamber. I'm sure y'all wouldn't want to hear it."

"I'll bet she would!" Sal said.

Gabe added, "If I'm in the dead guy's room, you've gotta have a good story for my sister's room."

"Do we dare tell it, Sal?" Camilla asked.

"Oh, yes, ma'am!"

"Well, all right, if you insist." Of course, she was dying to spill the story anyway. "Legend has it that Daphne—or maybe one of the Brookes girls—hid something of great value in that room."

"Like what?" Gabe asked.

"No one knows, and nothing's turned up all these years, even after two remodels." She searched our faces to see if this had any impact. "Who's to say? But I doubt y'all will find anything."

Oh, yeah? Maybe I would, just to spite her.

"Now, people, little Sal will lead us back downstairs and I'll tell y'all a bit more about Daphne, about her ear."

"Is it *eerie*?" Gabe asked.

"Eerier than y'all would think," Camilla said, nudging us toward the stairs. We followed Sal down with Camilla's disembodied voice telling the story behind us. "That girl was quite an eavesdropper. A bad habit, don't you know, especially in those harsh days before the War."

At the bottom of the stairs, Camilla went on with the story. "Well, now, poor Daphne was caught one time too many with her ear to the parlor door. Judge Nethercott, I guess he had no choice but to teach her a hard lesson. He ordered her ear sliced clean off."

"No!" I slapped my hand to my ear.

"Wicked," Gabe said soberly.

"Oh my, yes." Camilla's voice was full of triumph; she'd spooked us again.

My stomach did a flip-flop, thinking of poor Daphne and the terrible pain she must have felt.

". . . and from that day on, Daphne wore a yellow turban pulled low over the hole where her ear once set tight against her head. But she never eavesdropped again, to be sure."

"Instead she just murdered three people," said Gabe, frowning. "I see the improvement."

Camilla frowned at Gabe. "Folks say Daphne was some kind of a hoodoo healer. A few doubting Thomases like you, they wonder was it an accident that those two babies and their mama died? Did she really think a few sprinkles of oleander, or maybe some drops of the sap, would get those little ones just sick enough to need her doctoring? More than likely, she meant to do in the whole family, to get even with the Judge for her ear being slashed off. Well, y'all will have to decide for yourselves, because she's just not telling us, is she?"

And with that we heard a *click,* and she blew out the candle, plunging us into total darkness!

Gabe patted the nearest wall for a light switch. When the two dim sconces came back on, Camilla and Sal were both gone.

Chapter Seven
Daphne

That girl Lila looked at me in the mirror so intent. I'm pretty sure she saw me looking back, but then the boy joked some about cleaning the mirror smudge, and her eye left me. That business about where the poor soldier fell dead by the door—I couldn't tell, was Lila just doing what she saw Sal do? I better keep my hawk-eyes on her, and when the time's right, if it gets to be, I'll tell her about the *bébés*.

First time Miss Amelia showed me that statue of the golden *bébés* upstairs in her room, well, I tell you, it took my breath away. Looked like those saints shadowed in the nooks of the Judge's chapel we went to for church. Miss Amelia's two *bébés* were hugging each other's necks, and they were matched so perfect like they were inside and outside a mirror. Could have stood them up next to a jelly jar, and they'd have been the same height. And those *bébés* had angel wings and were crusted over with more sparkles than I ever saw in my whole life. I thought they must be right straight out of Jerusalem, the city of gold Tante Drucilla was always singing on about. Heavy they were, too, heavy as lead. I could tell by how Miss Amelia's hand dipped when she stood them up on her palm.

All this happened way before Eulie came up to the house, when Miss Amelia still favored me. She took my finger and smoothed it along the fat little legs of one of the *bébés*, and when I took my finger back, I popped it in my mouth, like you just had to be able to taste something that fine.

"Daphne, listen carefully," Miss Amelia said. She'd clicked the lock of her room, holding the key tight in her hand. She had such little hands, for a grown woman, and streaked up with blue veins. Miss Amelia leaned her head toward me, whispering like we were in the habit of telling each other secrets, which we weren't, her being the missus and me being just me.

With that key pressed into the palm of her hand, she set the *bébés* back in a little leathery box. "These darlings are particularly special to my family. The Cambridges of Philadelphia, don't you know. Of course, you can't read, so you'll just have to take my word—one of these little angels has my name on it, see? Amelia Maye. And the other has my sister's name, Ophelia Raye. She lived but a day, I'm sad to tell."

"Yes'm." Wasn't anything else I could answer.

Then she started saying things I didn't get the half of, but anyway they made the hairs on the back of my neck prickle up 'cause she wasn't altogether right in the head that night. Said, "Do you ever think about running away, Daphne?"

"No, ma'am!"

Running away's what the men down in the quarters were always chewing on when they'd sit around the fire drinking persimmon beer, letting the hope rise up like steam off a kettle. Each plan they hatched was wilder than the last one—ways to outsmart the patrollers—we called 'em pattyrollers, who made good money to hunt us down—and ways to put off the bloodhounds sniffing our scent. All right, but where would we go? How would we live? Nobody knew. And the plans never did amount to a tree with even the scrawniest fruit. Just like our little ones played "skip the stone," the men played "escape," to pass the time and keep their spirits from drying up like winter berries.

I wouldn't of gone, anyway. This was the only home I ever knew. Birdie was just like *ma mère*. Molly and Alice were my own sisters, even though I was more than twice Molly's age. And there was Isaac, who set my heart to tapping. So, when Miss Amelia asked, "Do you ever think about running away?" I could quick answer, "No, ma'am!" and be honest about it.

"Hear me clearly, Daphne. These babies are my family

history and my insurance policy if I ever need to, well, let us say, should I ever feel driven to return to my first home in Philadelphia. I was but a child younger than Molly when I came here. I was born a Yankee, don't you know."

"Yes, ma'am." Always telling me this, like there was some shame being born right here where Henriette birthed me.

She grabbed my arm then and pressed her bony fingers into my flesh. "And don't think of stealing my treasure, Daphne."

"I wouldn't do that, missus."

"Any of you Negroes would be strung up in a devil's minute if you got caught with something so valuable. Anybody who ever knew the Cambridges of Philadelphia would recognize my babies in an instant. So, if something should happen to me, I am entrusting you to look after them, Daphne. See that no harm comes to them, hear?"

"Yes'm." Why me, Lord?

"Living is dangerous, Daphne. We all come to the same end."

"Yes'm."

"My very own mother died in childbirth just as my third sister was born." She sighed deep enough to shake her shoulders. "Who knows what God, in His infinite judgment, calls us to? So, if by some rare stroke of fate you should outlive me, you're to come right to my room before my body's even cold, and hide this statue away for my daughters. It's *their* escape, should they need one. Every woman needs an escape plan, Daphne, just in case life gets too"—she took a while to find the right word, and

when she did, I didn't know what it meant—"too cumber-
some."

Felt like somebody tied a wrap around my head and
was pulling it tighter with every word. All I said was, "I'll
do my best, ma'am."

She looked at me good and hard, checking to see if I
was trusty. "Remember, I brought you up here to the house
when you were no older than my own Alice and taught you
to speak like a proper girl, or nearly," she reminded me, like
she did every time she wanted something special from me.
"And you're to tell no one about these cherubs—not Birdie,
who, mercy knows, has got ears all over this house, and not
Judge Nethercott either. Especially not the Judge. Promise,
Daphne?"

I promised but didn't even know what I was promising.

"One more thing, Daphne. God knows I'm alone here
with nobody to trust. You're my only hope, thin as it is."

That coulda been a compliment.

She sighed deep, then said, "All right, Daphne, I'll en-
trust you with this, even against my better judgment."

Probably wasn't a compliment.

"When the time is right, you're to make sure these
babies get into the proper hands."

"Whose hands, ma'am?"

"My daughters'. Didn't I make that abundantly clear?"
Patience wasn't what she was best at. "I do not have a window to the future. Nor do you, I suppose. But long after
I'm gone, someone must know I *lived,* Daphne, do you understand that?"

I understood, all right. Understood that I didn't understand a thing she had to say about those two *bébés* with the golden skin and eyes of green glass. But I promised, because if there's one thing I learned about working side by side with Birdie, it's to say *oui*, even if what you do is *non*.

Chapter Eight

Lila

Gabe and I scampered up the dark stairs after the candlelight tour. It was only nine-thirty, way too early to go to bed, and way too hot in our rooms, so we sat on the landing in the hall where a slight breeze cooled us about two degrees. Though Dad's snores shook the house, we whispered so we wouldn't wake up the parents. Besides, Laurel Oaks was beginning to feel like a place where you *had* to whisper. Not that I thought it was bugged; just that it felt like someone could be tuned in, listening to us.

"Okay, postmortem," I said, eager to get Gabe's view on the whole Camilla experience.

Gabe sat hunched up against the wall. He's a typical pitcher who spooks the batter by staring at him across the field, goes into a slow windup, then hurls a killer strike. My heart was practically caroming off the walls of my chest, waiting for the pitch, until I couldn't stand it any longer and I cried, "You saw the face in the mirror, didn't you, and the bloody drip marks?"

"I saw a bunch of black streaks. Simple explanation: someone scratched the silver stuff off the back of the mirror, and I don't believe for a minute that it's been replaced—what did she say? Nine times? Yeah, like anybody would really think that's dried blood? Come on!"

Okay, the mirror could have been just the power of suggestion. But the body on the floor? It yielded to my toes, soft and fleshy. I shuddered at the memory and asked, "What about the . . . thing at the bottom of the stairs, right in front of the door?"

Gabe shrugged. "Sal was faking, and you were going her one better, right? Camilla should put you in her show for tomorrow night."

"Gabe, I swear, something was there."

"Look, this place is rigged to make it seem like there's lots of *something there*." In his maddenly logical way, he continued. "We have all the props for your standard Halloween haunted mansion production, with the spooky house, scudding shadows, violent history, dripping blood, demented tour guide, and outrageous legends. Only thing missing is the creepy music."

"Yeah? But?"

"Yeah but nothing. I'm taking a shower."

I grabbed his arm. "Not yet. What about Sal? If this is all a Halloween monster house fake show, you think she's in on it?"

"Bingo." Gabe twirled his White Sox cap on his index finger, flinging it toward me like a Frisbee, the indoor game that drove our mom nuts. I hurled it down the stairs, barely missing the cat. Gabe ran down to retrieve the ball cap and put the cat outside again.

When he came back upstairs, I said, "I can't get Daphne out of my mind. Do you think she really murdered those two girls and their mother?"

"Hey, Lila! It's a legend. Get it? It's how they sell this place to gullible people who'll plunk down money for a good scare. Like going to a slasher movie."

"Well, yeah, maybe," I hedged, a little embarrassed. I grabbed the cap off his head and ran to the end of the hall with it. "Going out for a pass," I said, tossing it back to him. Bad aim; he stretched his leg out to try to catch it on his shoe, but it sailed past him, down the stairs again.

I curled up against the wall. I could hear something crackling under the wallpaper. Termites? Did they make sounds? Mice? That's all I needed!

Gabe bounded up the stairs two at a time, skipping number twelve, I noticed.

"Shh, the folks are sleeping," I warned. "Camilla and Sal, too."

"Not anymore!" he said, then sat there quietly for the longest time while the thought of mice skittering behind the wall goose-bumped me. Then the image of a knife slicing down the side of Daphne's head throbbed in the back of my eyes. I couldn't get the picture of her mangled ear out of my mind. Gabe sat a couple steps below me, with his ball cap crowning his knee.

"Since Roberto died . . ." I began.

"Roberto? What's he got to do with all this?" Gabe snapped. He'd kept all his feelings about Roberto's death under wraps, and now he changed the subject quickly. He sniffed under his arm. "Man, I really do need a shower."

I almost blurted the whole thing out about the midnight chanting and drumming since Roberto's death, but I stopped myself just in time. Gabe would wake up Dad and have me committed to the state hospital before sunrise!

Gabe yanked his shirt off; he *did* stink. I probably did, too. He asked brusquely, "Yeah, so, what about Roberto?"

"Nothing, nothing. I just think about him a lot, don't you? Especially here at Laurel Oaks."

"Here? Why?" Gabe took a baseball out of his shorts pocket and tossed the ball into the White Sox cap. The cap sagged with the weight of the ball. "You mean because Daphne's dead, and those people she killed are dead, and Roberto's dead, and there seems to be a lot of that ghost thing going around?" He waved his hands in front of my eyes. "Ooooooooh!" then sank back against the wall. "Roberto. No, I never think about him."

How was that possible? He'd been there when Roberto's family visited ours. He'd been to Jemez on Christmas and at Roberto's funeral. He'd carried little Lupita on his shoulders at the Balloon Fiesta just a week ago.

"Give me a break, Lila. It's all smoke and mirrors

around here, and I can't believe you're getting taken in by all that bogus stuff."

I hated when my brother thought I was stupid. I twirled the stud in my left ear, fighting back tears. "I'm really tired, Gabe. Let me have a turn in the bathroom before you take your shower."

He hit the stem on his watch. "I give you ninety seconds, and if you're not out by then, I'm sliding the ghost of Samuel Gladstone and a couple of his buddies under the door."

I left my bedroom door open and slid the window up to catch a breeze. Gazing out the window, I watched the narrow white slash of moon laced by branches and Spanish moss. Way off in the distance was a dim speck of flickering light, like maybe from a caretaker's cottage, or a neighboring plantation.

Something moved below my window! Not the cat. Too big for the cat. I heard a scraping sound like—what? The moon slid slowly out from behind the curtain of Spanish moss and shone right on a man below my window. He wore a white floppy hat, and he kept scraping a rake across the ground and dragging leaves into a pile, over and over. "Why would he be raking at ten o'clock at night?" I wondered aloud. He must have heard my voice. He stopped, looked up, and raised the rake to the moonlight. I dropped the curtain quickly and backed away from the window. Waited five minutes, then peeked through a narrow gap in the curtains.

The moon had shifted again, and he was gone.

A feeling of unease washed over me. I flopped down on my bed, listening to Gabe's shower water cranking its way through the ancient pipes and waited anxiously for him to come out of the bathroom. Ridiculous to be such a baby. I jumped up to close the door and rummaged through my backpack for a flashlight, then went back to lock the door. I lay on my back with the key buried under my pillow, and tried to make out details of the room through the gauzy mosquito netting: the antique vanity, the gold brocade love seat, the chandelier with its crystal teardrops tinkling in the occasional breeze, and some sort of needlepoint thing on the far wall.

Maybe I drifted off and dreamed, or maybe I had this weird vision rolling across the screen of my mind. . . . *An elegant lady flitting around in a hoop skirt hovering an inch above the floor. A servant comes into the parlor with a glass bell to call everyone in to dinner, and the lady glides into that horrid dining room where the poisoning would happen, holding a little girl by each hand.*

The picture came through so clearly that I was virtually in the room feeling the stifling heat, and smelling roasted mutton, yeasty rolls, and whiskey-soaked bread pudding. *Don't eat the cake!!!!!*

A slave girl stands at the foot of the table operating a hand-cranked giant sweeping fan that cools the guests and keeps flies from dropping into the glass bowls of wild raspberries. The girl looks hot and bored. She runs a long, graceful finger under the edge of a yellow turban to loosen it from where it's pasted to the side of her face with her own sweat. It hangs at an awkward angle over one ear.

Daphne!

I bolted up and panned my flashlight around to dispel the image. I did *not* want Daphne in my head. Light, light would clear things up.

Get a grip! I told myself. I refused to give in to this out-of-control feeling.

Sleep sounded tasty. It would clear my head so I'd wake up, have a good breakfast, and explore Laurel Oaks in the cool reality of daylight. Sleep, that's what I needed. No drumming, no Indian chants, no mice, no cats. No ears.

I pulled the lamp chain—pitch-black—and fell asleep to the buzzing and the singsong chirping of the crickets.

Chapter Nine
Daphne

That family staying here, I'd watched the father fumbling around with the locks, cursing under his breath, turning the keys every which way until his wife got it right. That put me in mind of Birdie telling me about the keyholes.

"Birdie," I asked her once, "why's it the keyholes in the house are put in upside down?" Now, how would I know that, coming up in the quarters where we had no keys, because we had no locks on our splintery old shacks, and nothing to lock up, anyway. Only way I'd know is, a Yankee from way up north came by the house one day, came riding up in a one-horse wagon loaded down with all manner of goods. I had my eye on some material for a mantua Birdie promised to sew me up. "Child, time you had a growed-up dress and apron," she said.

That bolt of material in his wagon just about jumped out at me. It was as yellow as churned butter, and I wanted it so bad that spit was pooling in my mouth like a running faucet. I suspected Isaac was partial to yellow, since he took care of the Judge's horses, and he dearly favored the yellow mare named Candlewax.

I tell you, Miss Amelia bought that whole bolt, and three or four of us had yellow church dresses from it before the summer tomatoes pinked up. But, I was saying about the keyholes. That peddler, he noticed the lock on the tea safe when Birdie brought him into the kitchen for some sweet tea.

He rolled the cool glass across his wrinkly forehead and said, "Well, I'll be. I see your keyholes are upside down, ladies. Now, isn't that an interesting fact? I'll venture a wild guess. I'll wager it's because you're south of the Mason-Dixon line, right? Up north of the line, we put in our keyholes right side up."

Birdie swiped at a pool of sweat that had dripped off his pointy beard onto her biscuit rolling table. "Who says which way's up and which way ain't? Just a way of turning your key." She grabbed the glass out of the poor man's hand and showed him the door.

I could tell she was holding something back, so I asked when his wagon raised dust behind it, "Birdie, why *are* Miss Amelia's keyholes upside down?"

"Ain't you smart enough to figure that out, with the schooling I been giving you?"

"Hunh-uh, don't guess I am."

She fingered that pretty yellow material, sizing me up with one eye squinted. "Keep out the evil spirits, the haunts. Spirits can slip through the keyholes if they ain't set in just so. Even white folks know that."

Now, those spirits, they're different from the Holy Spirit the priest, Père Jacques, was always preaching about in church, but truth to tell, I don't know just how it was different. Good, I guess, not evil. Ooh, but there were lots of stories about evil spirits back when I was a girl. The griots, the storytellers, brought all kinds of tales with them from Africa, about spirits and witches and whammies, and we told them over and over. After me and Birdie cleaned up the kitchen real good, I'd sometimes go down to the quarters to visit the *tantes*. Tante Drucilla'd be finishing her washing up, swishing water around her cook pot, and she'd say, "Mind, you and me'd best keep an eye on that Eulie. She's a witch if I ever did see one. She's got something to prove, but Lord knows what. Say, I ever tell you about when I get that itchy feeling, just like the Queen of Sheba, my great-great-grand?"

"Only about a hundred times!" I'd tell her with a chuckle.

"Well, I'm getting it now, sure as I've got flesh to scratch," she'd say. "You and Eulie are fighting over something, can't guess what, and only the Lord Hisself knows which one of you is s'pose to win the fight."

Nowadays, I think about that a lot. Sure enough, Eulie is up to her old tricks again, like in the days of Miss Amelia when Eulie was always slipping out of her skin and into a cat's to claw and ride good folks until they woke up aching something awful. How do I know that's what she was up to so long ago? Because, having such a busy time, night after night, she'd drag herself like a sack of bones into the kitchen in the mornings, even though we had horseshoes hanging over each door to keep out witches. I tell you, I'd have to dodge all around Eulie to get breakfast on the table for the family, 'cause she was about as useless as a roach.

I don't know, maybe she's got something against that Lila girl. I do know this, though. There's only one way to outsmart a witch, and that's to sprinkle salt and pepper on her empty skin before she can slip back into it at sunup. I'd of done it to Eulie if I'd been able to catch her at just the right time, 'cause a witch can't crawl into a salt-and-peppery skin. Without it, she'd be nothing but a shadow spirit, wandering the place forever and a day. She'd never cross the River Jordan, like Père Jacques tells about, to make it to the promised land.

Well, I'm no witch, but I'm hungering for a corner of the promised land myself after way more than a hundred years without any skin to live in.

Can't rest, though, until the golden *bébés* are safe in somebody's hands. I promised Miss Amelia, didn't I? A woman's word is good as money under the bedroll. You can count on it even if it costs you more than you think you got to give, like her angel *bébés* did me.

Chapter Ten

Lila

It seemed like I'd slept for hours, days, but when my eyes snapped open, my cell phone said it was just 12:28 A.M. I peeked out around an opening in the mosquito net. The room was still and full of dark shadows. Where was the moon hiding? The only light was a thin strip under my door from the lamp in the hall.

I tiptoed out there, watching for the cat, but I guess she'd found somewhere to curl up and sleep for the night. Lucky cat.

Dad opened his and Mom's door. "Thought I heard someone out here." His bed-hair sprouted all over his head, and he had a crease on his cheek. "You okay, honey?" he asked.

"Yes, sure." The tiny shred of little girl left in me wanted to jump into bed between Mom and Dad, like both of us kids used to do on tornado watch nights back when we lived in Kansas. "I'm okay, Dad," I assured him. "Just on my way to the bathroom for a pit stop."

"All right, sleep tight, don't let—"

"Yeah, yeah, I know, the bed bugs bite." I kissed Dad's cheek and waited until his door was shut, then tiptoed back into my own room and locked the door.

Even through the curtains, even through the gauzy mosquito netting, the room was suddenly brightened by a harsh moon that had popped out from behind the clouds. I fluffed up my pillows to study every dark corner, every shadow. Vigilant against—what? I was glad this wasn't one of the rooms the Nethercott girls had died in.

My eyes drifted shut, then snapped open again. Across the room I could almost believe that my backpack on the love seat was a body, and that the Tiffany lamp beside it was a severed head. On the other side of the room the coat-rack topped by that antique hat was a hangman's scaffold, ready for the drop. And that lethal hat pin . . .

No! Can't think that way! I oriented myself to the four winds, like the Jemez Indians do, then remembered a folk superstition I'd read in some short story at school: never sleep crosswise of the world, with the bed going north and south. Safe—this bed was positioned east to west. Or was it? Which direction had the sun set that afternoon? My thinking was fuzzy, frizzy around the edges.

I slid down a couple of inches, forced my eyes to pull wide open. No apparitions, no strange ectoplasmic blobs floating in the air. Even the insects outside seemed to be holding their breath. In fact, the whole house lay weirdly silent, and the silence lulled me into daydreaming. I jarred myself alert, then made my racing pulse slow to a steady whomp, whomp.

An owl screeched.

I bolted up in bed. The room smelled of age and lavender and something else I couldn't place. Everything looked murky, like I was viewing it underwater again. I remembered: mosquito netting was draped over the bedposts, billowing in the breeze of the useless air-conditioning.

Just minutes ago, when I was fighting sleep, the air had been eerily silent, but suddenly the house intensified the insect riot outside and magnified every creak of the floorboards. Even the light in the hall gave off a faint crackling sound, as if the bulb might shatter any second. *Don't let the light go out. The spirits . . .*

The owl screeched again. A screeching owl signals death. I must have read that somewhere.

It's just a bird, I told myself. I'm safe in here. The door's locked. Gabe and Mom and Dad are across the hall, a holler away. And Roberto? Dead and buried. It was just an owl. Just an ugly bird.

Okay, heart, quit hammering. Lungs, breathe, breathe, in steady rhythm. There.

Soft footsteps.

Was I dreaming? Someone was lifting the mosquito netting!

A scream froze in my throat; I couldn't move a muscle as a dark face peered down at me. Moonlight painted the girl's face and the odd yellow cap pulled to one side of her head. Black eyes drilled into my own, begging something, but what?

A shimmery, hoarse voice filled my mind, yet there was no sound in the room. Just the words, the terrible words in my head:

Find the babies in the wall . . . the babies in the wall . . . the babies.

And then the netting wafted down, brushing across my cheeks like the fluttering wings of a bird, and the girl with the yellow turban vanished.

Poof.

The next morning I woke to the sound of a rooster crowing and a dash of light poking through the gap in the curtains. I sat up in bed and stretched, tossing aside the mosquito netting. Six A.M. Normal people were still asleep, but how, with that nonstop crowing? "Okay, okay, I get the message, rooster. I'm rising, but not shining, so you can shut up." This was more thought than I'd given to chickens in my entire life, unless they were on my dinner plate.

I felt vaguely uneasy. Something about a dream, something that happened during the night, but I couldn't remember even a fragment of it, as though I'd totally disappeared into the blackness.

Sunshine gradually seeped into the room. The rooster kept crowing, but distant now, like a far-off train whistle. The shifting light slanted across that needlepoint sampler thing hanging on the wall. I craned my neck to give it a better look, squinting in the rosy glow gathering in the room. I went over to examine the sampler more closely. It was dated 1832, which made it fifteen or twenty times my age. For some reason, it creeped me out. I resisted the urge to turn its face to the wall. Instead, I studied the reds and blues and yellows that must have been bright and pretty a long time ago. Somebody—maybe that mother who died of poisoning—had been careful to hand-stitch a sappy poem. I started reading it out loud:

*Fragrant The Rose Is,
But It Fades In Time . . .*

"Yeah, so did the colors," I said out loud.

Daylight. Things were normal again. I opened my window and breathed in the swamp soup that Louisiana called air. How could it be so hot and thick at six in the morning? I quickly yanked my head back in. My eyes swept the room again. That ugly chandelier I'd heard tinkling in the night hung from the center of the ceiling, with gold and crystal cherubs suspended by their feet, their faces staring down toward me. Kind of disturbing, like that Fragrant Rose sampler. In fact, the whole room made my skin itch.

The rooster wouldn't give up. You'd think he'd have had laryngitis already. I'd cheerfully have wrung his neck if I could catch him, and then I'd feed him to that cat with the yellow eyes. They deserved one another!

The wonderful smell of bacon wafted up through the A/C vent, along with muffled voices. I was suddenly hungry enough to eat a horse. A door slammed downstairs, then I heard a loud, "YES, MA'AM!" I opened my window again and saw Sal running the length of the gallery.

"Sal! Hey, good morning!" I called down to her.

She stopped in her tracks and looked up at me. "Morning, ma'am."

"I'm no ma'am. I'm Lila. The rooster wake you up, too? I'll bet you're heading for the barn to collect eggs from those hens."

"No chickens here," Sal said. "Had of been, Miss Camilla would of scared 'em off."

No rooster? That was strange, but then the crowing had stopped. "Wait there, Sal, I want to talk to you." I slipped a T-shirt over my pj tank top and ran down to Sal.

We sat on the rockers. She had to scoot to the edge of the seat so her feet would reach the ground.

"So Camilla's not your mother?" I asked.

"Her? Sheesh. Just my foster 'til somethin' better turns up."

"What happened to your parents?"

"My mama, she passed before I lost my first tooth." Sal spread her lips to show me a mouthful of very large teeth crisscrossing each other like weeds. "My grandmama reared me up three, four years after that, but she's bent over with the osteo-authoritis thing, and that's how I come here, to Miss Camilla. She needs somebody like me," Sal said with a chuckle.

"What about your father?"

"My daddy, he never really was one."

"Oh, I thought maybe that gardener was your father."

"Gardener who?"

"The one I saw last night, raking in the moonlight."

"Ain't no gardener here. Miss Camilla, she has a yard service comes once a week, but Thursday ain't his time. Anyway, he don't come nights."

"But I saw . . ." *No, I didn't see him.*

"Guess you must be talking about that ghost, old Luke. Some folks spot him around here, but I never do. What's he look like?"

Ghost? "It was dark, and I couldn't see him clearly." Crazy. I was actually talking to this girl about a *ghost*.

Sal leaned back with bare feet straight out like planks. Her toenails were painted purple with yellow dots.

"You seen *her*, didn't you?"

My heart stopped.

"Daphne, last night," Sal said.

Fragments of the dream, if it was a dream, trickled back into my consciousness. Something about . . . babies. Find the babies? "I think so," I whispered. "How did you know?"

"Sal! Come here this instant!" Camilla called. "We've got breakfast to do, and the school bus'll be here before you know it. You don't dare miss another day of school, or they'll put you back in third grade!"

Sal jumped out of the rocker, sending it thumping. "Ain't she just a bucket of pure joy?" she said, running off.

Chapter Eleven

Lila

When I reached the top of the stairs, I found Gabe standing in the hall with a pink rosebud towel knotted at his waist.

I burst out laughing. "Very cute. Lock yourself out?"

"You think it's funny?" he grumbled. "I had to send Dad down to find Camilla, who seems to live in the sub-terranean bowels of the house."

"Shh, here she comes."

Camilla trudged up the stairs behind Dad, jangling her set of jailor's keys. When she spotted Gabe dripping on her carpet, she said, "Y'all ought to be carrying your room keys."

Gabe imitated Sal's overly polite, "Yes, ma'am, but see? There's no pocket in this towel."

"Gabriel," Dad warned.

Camilla unlocked his door and gave us a snarly *hmph* on her way downstairs.

Dad was in his usual striped polo shirt and khakis baggy at the knees, looking his geeky self, and that was reassuring. Normal, predictable. "You kids have a good night? I only woke up once when I heard you in the hall, Lila. After that, Mom and I slept like lambs."

"Sure, great, Dad." *Except for a few dead people popping up in my dreams.*

"There's breakfast in the General Store, but it's store-bought muffins," Dad said scornfully. Always the foodie snob. "I'll spring for a hearty breakfast and a look-around in the town, then we'll run your mother over to Baton Rouge. How does a stack of blueberry pancakes sound?"

Delicious, and I was ready to leave Laurel Oaks for a while and go where everybody was *alive.*

St. Francisville turned out to be roughly the size of my school campus. A main drag café seemed to be *the* place to go, judging by how many people were pouring out the door waiting for a table. A biker couple had just parked their Harleys nearby and got in line, in the middle of an argument about a storm. She said, "Booley-babe, I'm thinking we scrap the trek to N'Awlins. I'm not up for getting drenched to my drawers."

Booley apparently was, because he said, "We're goin', see? Since when's a little storm spooked you?"

"A storm?" I asked. "You mean like a hurricane?"

"Nah," the guy said. "Just a high pressure system that'll prob'ly dump buckets on us. Heavy winds howling in from the west."

Gabe asked skeptically, "Are you a TV weatherman?"

He sure didn't look like one, with the belly hanging over his black jeans and the orange skull dangling from one earlobe.

"Nah, just a storm-chaser, but Janey here's a wuss."

Janey-here rammed him an elbow jab to that flabby roll over his belt buckle. Twirling a hank of her own black frizzy hair, she pointed to my spikes and said, "Great-looking locks, girl. Use axle grease to keep it perked up straight like that?"

"Yak butter," I said.

"Way cool."

Mom and Dad exchanged one of their typical puzzled looks, then Mom said, "Ethan, are you all right driving to Baton Rouge in the deluge?" We're from Albuquerque, land of desert drought and grit.

Before Dad could respond, Booley turned to Mom and said, "Storm's not coming through until, like, four o'clock. You got time, lady. B'sides, a little wind and rain never hurt anybody."

I was amazed. "How can you say that, after Katrina?"

Booley just shrugged, which sent his skull earring spinning.

Eventually we got a table, but the café was so noisy that Gabe and I could just tune out of the conversation. Good, because I didn't want Mom and Dad asking a lot of questions, and I sure didn't have any answers.

The buckwheat hotcakes were heavenly, with straw-
berries and whipped cream heaped on top. Everyone else
had three shrunken brown logs of sausage on their plates,
but I'm a vegetarian. Sort of. About every three weeks I'm
obsessed with the need for a hunk of meat, and tofu veg-
gie burgers just don't do it.

I gulped down the last of my pulpy orange juice. We
gave up our table to people hovering over us, and checked
out the little town. Mom stayed in the car to polish her
presentation while Dad and Gabe and I stopped into the
one-room historical museum chockful of Feliciana Parish
history. I found out Louisiana has parishes, not counties
like regular states do.

Dad had to read every word on every exhibit, and I
did my usual museum run-through number, until Gabe
said, "Over here, Lila, it's our buddy."

I ducked around an exhibit board to see what he'd
found. A large black-and-white photo leaned against the
back of a glass case. The picture was fuzzy, like a poor
reproduction from Kinko's. I recognized the corner of
Laurel Oaks, joining the back of the house and the General Store, and there in the corner stood a figure, a young
woman. Her dress was long and dark, very old-fashioned,
and she leaned against a white post, one arm bracing
her as if she'd just staggered out of the house. Her hair
was swathed in a turban. Below the picture the caption
read:

MANY CONTEMPORARY PHOTOGRAPHERS
HAVE CAPTURED THIS IMAGE, THOUGHT TO

BE DAPHNE, THE FIFTEEN-YEAR-OLD SLAVE
GIRL WHO, AS THE LEGEND TELLS, POISONED
AMELIA MAYE CAMBRIDGE NETHERCOTT
AND HER TWO LITTLE GIRLS IN 1839.

"How weird is that!" said Gabe. "Somebody saying he
actually captured her image? Man, I'd like to know what
kind of film that guy used." He glanced over at me. "Aw,
you're not thinking it's really her, are you?"

With my heart thudding, my knees weak, I couldn't
drag my eyes away from the picture. I recognized her. The
whole dream, or vision, or whatever it was, streamed back
through my mind. *Find the babies.*

"Yes, it's Daphne," I said. She was leaning against the
post; I leaned against the glass case, my head spinning. "I
saw her, Gabe. Last night."

"You *saw* her? The girl's been dead for, what? A hundred and seventy years, and you *saw* her?"

I nodded, trembling.

"You let that stupid tour last night get to you, Lila.
Give it up!"

"I know what I saw," I said firmly.

"Get real, Lila. Jeez, your imagination's in super-
overdrive." He glared at me, surprising me with his anger.
But he wasn't done. "Crazy talking about Roberto, and the
ear thing, and the poisoning, and that body at the front
door, which incidentally wasn't *there*. Pull yourself together, or I'm telling Dad."

Just then Dad came around the exhibit board. "We've

got to get going, kids." He looked closely at me, then at the picture of Daphne and the caption. He must have picked up on the steam coming off Gabe and me and asked, "What's going on here?"

Gabe said quickly, "Just some Laurel Oaks flimflam stuff. All part of the spectacle."

"Anything I should be concerned about? Mom and I are experienced fretters. It's part of our job description." We shook our heads. "Ready to go, then? Your mother's going to be late to her conference if we don't get a move on."

Mom saved Dad from a bunch of wrong turns, while Gabe and I sat in the backseat stewing the whole way to Baton Rouge and never said a word to each other.

At the university, we pulled up next to a giant palm tree, in front of the sprawling Health Sciences Center where Mom's conference was to be held.

"I'll pick you up right here, Emily. Four-thirty okay?"

Mom gathered up a bulky canvas bag and her small leather backpack and opened the car door. Another blast from the familiar Louisiana oven hit us. "Have a great day, everybody!" she said, sliding out of the car to join the stream of people filing into the building.

I was relieved when Gabe jumped out of the car and moved up front with Dad. Naturally, Dad got turned around on campus, and we drove into lots of dead ends. At home, he could get lost in the Albertson's parking lot.

Once we found our way back on the road, he said, "I'd like to take the ferry from Bayou Sarah across the narrow neck of the Mississippi. There's a French town called New

Roads over there, and I've made an appointment to interview a chef at Satterfields, that famous crawfish étouffée
restaurant." Dad was always hunting down quirky chefs
and local grub. "So, do you want to come, or do you want
me to drop you back at the plantation?"

"Plantation," Gabe and I said together, but maybe for
different reasons. We'd been to a few of Dad's boring chef
interviews, with the white-hat guys showing off in French
and Italian, and Dad taking notes in a frenzy of flipping
papers. That was probably Gabe's reason, but I was chomp-
ing to get back to the house. Too much had happened; too
much with too little explanation.

"Your choice," Dad said. "I'll only be a couple of hours,
and we can go have lunch, and then I'll pick up your mother
after the conference, for dinner."

Dad's life was organized into three perfect meals a
day, lots of them tax deductible because of his work. Three
squares a day—about as concrete and down-to-earth as
any human being could get. He'd never see a ghost if one
walked up and smooched him on the lips.

He turned up the radio and hummed along to Creole
zydeco with lots of cheesy accordion. Not my style. But at
least the music made it impossible for Gabe and me to talk
all the way back to St. Francisville.

Deep in my bones I felt that something major waited
for us there, but I wasn't at all sure I wanted to meet it
face-to-face.

Chapter Twelve
Daphne

That time last night, it was the first I ever told a living soul about the *bébés*, except *mon cher* Isaac, but that was before I passed. A whole many years have gone by. And I'm thinking, Miss Amelia trusted me with those *bébés*, and I turned out to be the wrong one to trust. Same thing gonna happen with me and Lila? I was hoping she'd be ready to hear from me direct. So, I pulled back that mosquito net. Her eyes were wide open, taking all of it in. But sometimes when daylight comes, folks don't believe what they know happened in the night. Well, all I can do now's wait-see what she does and pray Eulie doesn't mess things up too bad.

Long time back, I swear, Eulie was getting more uppity the longer she fritted around in Birdie's kitchen. She had a heart dry as old wood. Said, "I s'pose you're running to tend to all them folks down in the quarters like you're tethered to them."

Birdie gave her a slashy look. "Mind them ducks, child. Judge likes 'em crisp on the outside, tender inside, which is more'n I can say for you. And you just leave me to do my calling."

She was always messing things up for Birdie and me. Oh, I do so miss Birdie.

Birdie could sew stitches small as dots on both sides. If you blackened the right side of an apron with coal dust so it wouldn't wash clean, or spotted it with lard, you could turn it inside out, and the wrong side would look as good as the right. She did that close-up work with little spectacles that slid around on the sweat of her nose. They used to be Miss Amelia's specs 'til she got stronger ones for reading. I don't know how *anybody* could see such small scratchings as there were on Miss Amelia's books, and make sense of 'em.

My Alice always had her nose in a book, too, twisting a string of her silky hair all the while she read. I liked when she read to Molly, 'cause I'd listen to the story and act like I was just brushing Molly's snarly hair, or polishing the chiffonier in the parlor.

The chiffonier—that was my favorite piece of furniture, and maybe it's crazy to be so partial to a big piece of wooden cabinetry. What I liked about it was the mirror on the breakfront, way down low to the floor.

"Funny spot to place a mirror," I once said to Birdie, and she told me what it was for. So the ladies could check to be sure their unders didn't hang down longer than their dress. I stood there in front of that mirror whenever I had an idle minute, because it showed my ankles. My ankles were the best part of my whole self, and especially when Isaac gave me a piece of string dyed red to tie around my left-hand foot. He wore one, too, on his right. "Ties us together," he said. Such a sweet-talker, Isaac. He didn't dare fix it on my ankle himself, though, because if Birdie'd caught us—well, she didn't have a bit of problem about turning her grown boy over her knee for a licking, him being her youngest.

Birdie had an abroad marriage. That means her husband lived on a different plantation. They only got together two, three times a year, and she didn't go looking at any other men while they were apart, either. She was real particular about courting, especially me courting. Especially Isaac. She thought I didn't hear what she said to Isaac, but I was always listening where I shouldn't of. Said, " 'Til you two's man and wife, you keep your hands in your pockets. And you ain't gonna be man and wife 'til I says so. Daphne hardly ain't ripe yet."

Wish the Judge had heard that. I wish he thought about it all those nights he came calling with his lantern swinging in the dark of my corner by the stove. "I've come for warmth," he always said, though his eyes were cold and he left me shivering and freezy as the midnight river.

Ketty came running to the house one day, pulling at her pigtails and bellowing like a stuck pig. "Birdie, come quick! Eulie's Tom ain't gone live through the night if his *maman* have her way!"

Birdie said to me over her shoulder, "That Eulie. Got chicken feed for brains," then said with a big sigh for Ketty's ears, "That girl just ain't right in the head when *Papa le Bas* come on her." The devil, for sure.

Birdie knew just what to do, because poor Tom, about old as me, he'd called on her more than once before. So Birdie grabbed up an oak bucket and pulled me by the sleeve, and we dipped the bucket in the well out back for cool spring water. Birdie prayed and worried over that water until, I swear, ripples started rising on it like the river current was fixing for a storm.

We ran down to Eulie's shack, sloshing water. No sign of Anjou, that good-for-nothing man of hers, but Eulie was chasing her boy Tom around the place, leaping on the bedrolls and the table, slamming an iron skillet at the air. Poor Tom held his hands up to keep from getting his teeth knocked across the room. Wasn't going to be good for the frying pan, either.

Birdie grabbed Eulie by the apron strings and eased her down off the table. Then, right before my eyes, a different Birdie came over her. Her eyes locked on Eulie, her mouth set in a straight line, her back stretched taller than when she reached up to the highest shelf in her kitchen. Her voice went low and slow, hardly more than a whisper in Eulie's ear. Tom just watched all wide-eyed, and him with no hair 'cause of the ringworm.

Birdie motioned for me to put the dipper into the bucket and to lift a cupful to Eulie's lips. Eulie caught my eyes, and seemed like the temperature dropped to shivers in that messy shack of hers. She whipped her face away from the dipper.

"Ain't taking nothing from *her!*"

Well, lots of folks down there had no use for me, and why? Because up at the house I got plenty of meat and apple dumplings for breakfast if I wanted them, and a thick straw mattress over behind the stove, even if I didn't get it all to myself.

"She's living like a lady," I'd heard Eulie sputter to Ketty one time. "Before you know it, her skin be bleach-white, just like that uppity free man, Luke Mullin. Both be white as ghosts!"

"Miss Amelia's pet," they said, "Judge's lap dog," they said. And worse.

Now Birdie gave Eulie a look that could rip thorns right off a rosebush. Told her, "Daphne's been learning to doctor, so you just give yourself over to her, you hear, child?" She turned Eulie's face so she had to look me in the eye. Birdie showed me how to hold my hand under Eulie's flabby chin to catch the drips. Said, "Cool, fresh water, child. Drink of it," over and over, until Eulie took a swallow, even out of my hand. I watched it jiggle down her throat, some of it pooling up under a couple of her chins. In a minute, her shoulders sagged, giving up the fight. That pan she was clutching hit the dirt floor with a clattery thud.

Tom kicked the pan aside and moved in closer, put his hand on Eulie's shoulder, said, "*Maman*?"

We left Eulie and her boy to their sweet time, and on the way to the big house, Birdie said, "I fixed the hush water for Tom. His mama ain't gonna nag or worry him with a fry pan for a good long while."

"Did I do all right, Birdie?" meaning, can you make somebody unsick if it's somebody you hate with your whole heart?

"Important thing is, Eulie done took it from you."

Not long after that I put my one ear to the parlor door when Miss Amelia and the Judge were having a fight. Wasn't a spitfire fight like Eulie and her boy. The Judge and Miss Amelia, theirs was a fight with words so icy, they left me with the fever-shivers.

She told the Judge, "A little bit of knowledge is a dangerous thing, Mr. Nethercott." She was saying, without saying it, that she knew where he went with his lantern, barefoot at night. And she was warning, without warning him, that she planned to do something about it, all right. That something had to do with Eulie, 'cause she knew how me and Eulie felt about each other. Funny thing, as much as Miss Amelia and the Judge acted like we didn't have eyes or ears and we were all as invisible as air, Miss Amelia always seemed to know what was going on between us. Just like the folks down in the quarters were jealous of me having the comforts of the house, I think

Miss Amelia was jealous of how Birdie and me were close as roosting hens. Plain to see, the Judge wouldn't be the one getting the frying pan like poor Tom would of. I was the one, and it'd come down on me soon enough. Miss Amelia was too refined a lady, a *Philadelphia lady*, even though she barely lived a year of her life as a Yankee, to slap a hand on me, but oh, Lord, how she could crush the spirit.

Chapter Thirteen

Lila

By the time Dad dropped Gabe and me off at Laurel Oaks that morning, we'd reached enough of a truce to park ourselves opposite each other on stone benches outside the house. Sweat ran down my neck and T-shirt. My palms were sweaty, too, but not because of the humidity. I plunged into The Subject. "I have to tell you something, Gabe. Don't yell, don't go off in a snit, and don't tell me I'm stark-raving mad. Just listen, okay?"

Gabe tossed his baseball from hand to hand like a Slinky. "I'm listening."

"I swear something happened last night. I saw Daphne in my room."

"Like you told me. You mean in a dream, right?"

"Not a dream. Well yes, at first, I guess." I thought of the dream? vision? of the Laurel Oaks dining room, back in the days when Daphne was a servant. "But later, I'm totally serious, she was *there*. She opened the mosquito netting and looked right at me."

Gabe palmed the ball and took a deep breath. "Don't take it personally, and don't get mad at me, either, but I'm finding this way hard to believe. I mean, considering that you're alive, and she's dead."

"I know, but it happened."

"Okay," he said with a sigh. "What did she look like?" Humoring me.

"A little older than you, maybe fifteen. Small, dark features. Pale sort of beige lips, very dry and cracked. She kept licking them. Black bullet eyes, but sad eyes, pleading eyes." I stopped, to solidify the details in my own mind. "She had something on her head."

"Yeah, that doo-wrap thing."

"Camilla called it a turban. Real sweaty-looking and wilted and full of holes. She wore it at an odd angle, too, pulled over one side of her head."

"We know what *that's* about," Gabe added, yanking at his ear.

Was he beginning to get it? "I swear, she looked just like the image in the mirror."

"Which I didn't see."

"And in that museum picture."

He let out another deep sigh, reaching for patience, which irritated me.

"You think I'm having hallucinations like a schizo, don't you?"

"I didn't say that." Gabe stretched, clasping the ball in both hands over his head.

"You didn't have to. But you don't believe any of this stuff is really happening." I looked across at him, silently pleading for his support.

He took his usual long time to answer. "I believe that *you* believe it's all happening, and for now, that's the best I can do. Okay, better tell me, what did Daphne want with you?"

I answered honestly. "She wants me to find the babies."

"What babies?"

"In the wall," I said miserably. "She's desperate for me to find them."

"Babies? Aw, jeez, Lila. I'm really trying, but this makes no sense."

"Everything doesn't have to make sense. Some things just *are*."

"Yeah, but this whole Daphne thing is more than I can swallow."

"I'm not nuts, Gabe. You've got to believe me."

"Whoa, I'm outta my league here."

"Gabe, I know you don't like to talk about Roberto."

"Nothing to talk about," he muttered.

"There is. You just can't face it." How far could I go

with this? Tears sprang to my eyes, and I took the plunge. "I think Roberto's trying to reach me."

"From beyond the grave, right." Gabe slammed the ball to the ground with a thud.

"I hear him chanting, I hear his drums . . ."

Gabe jumped to his feet and kicked the ball into a clump of bushes. "I can't deal with this, Lila. I just can't. I've gotta take off for a while to do some thinking."

"Go ahead," I said, pouting. "I need a break from you, too." I folded my arms across my chest and spun around on the bench, with my back to him. I heard his sneakers flap against the concrete walkway as he took off, leaving me sorely disappointed. I'd so much hoped he'd understand about the weird things that were happening to me. How could I convince him? I needed proof. Sal? Maybe I could find the raking man, the one Sal said was a ghost, and get him to stick around long enough that Gabe could talk to him.

I watched my brother sprint through the grass. He was the fastest runner on his team, clocked at three seconds from first base to second. Dashing across the open Laurel Oaks field was a cinch, even if it did look a little like a thick jungle.

I walked aimlessly through the grounds, looking for something, but I had no idea what it was. After about ten minutes I was dripping quarts of sweat, even in the shade, so I dropped down into wilted grass and leaned against the front porch railing of the mansion. I tried to clear the clutter out of my mind and let it drift, to keep it open to what I was meant to find there at Laurel Oaks. Whatever it was.

I blinked, forcing my eyes open, because I sensed someone out there, and it wasn't Gabe. For a split second I thought it was Roberto. Impossible, but even if it was, he quickly morphed into a different figure. Did I conjure him up through pure will? I don't know, but suddenly a man was there drawing leaves into a pile that never grew any taller.

I stood up and crept closer to him, burning with determination to get a good look at him. His skin was dark and pitted, sprouting gray whiskers. Worn overalls covered a plaid shirt, with one shoulder strap undone. A huge sweat-stained white hat flopped around his face and ropy neck.

"Hello?" I called out timidly. No response. He seemed to be looking *at* me and *away* at the same time—cross-eyed. I turned to follow his gaze. Nothing there but a tree. In the split second that I studied the tree, the figure vanished in a puff of dust, the way Daphne had the night before. Oh, great. Now it was happening in the daylight.

I wandered over to the tree, the tallest one in the front of the house. Live oak, I guessed, by the leaves that were shaped like fat feathers and just turning into autumn-gold. The trunk was huge, maybe ten feet in diameter, tapering into skinnier branches higher up with lots of places for squirrels to nest. I scampered up a few limbs. Sometimes it pays to be a tomboy, even though my bare knees were scraping raw on the rough bark.

I eyeballed and patted the tree as far up as I could

reach. It felt very comfortable, very comforting. I climbed higher. A little risky. The limbs were thinner, maybe wouldn't support me. Was that a voice I heard? I leaned my ear toward the closest branch and heard a humming sound that seemed to come from the tree trunk itself. My heart began to pound. All at once I felt my senses spring sharply into focus. I smelled the sweet sap of the tree, heard its leaves rustling. My legs brushed its shaggy bark. I'd never felt this way before, both intensely, wholly alert, and drowsily drifting.

Roberto. I dreamed him, or daydreamed him, or imagined him—everything was so mixed up. All I know is that Roberto came to mind, and it was about that last Christmas when the four of us Barrys went to the Jemez Pueblo. We were wrapped in jackets and scarves and mittens until there wasn't a square inch of skin exposed for the hours we watched the dancing in the plaza.

Men and boys in eagle feathers or buffalo hide swooped around the center plaza, legs pumping. Women and girls danced from foot to foot with bells on their white boots and gourd rattles in their hands. Their brightly colored skirts and headdresses billowed in the west wind. I felt very plain in my navy parka and blue jeans.

This dancing was deeply spiritual to the Jemez, at least that's what Roberto had told us, but it wasn't for us outsiders to know just *what* it meant, so to us it was like a circus parade or a pageant that you couldn't help loving every minute of.

Not Gabe. He was restless after half an hour and hung out with some of the Jemez boys who were eating sunflower seeds and tossing the husks onto the pink dirt. Dad swayed to the chanting in his usual two-beats-behind way, and Mom-the-anthropologist, with her hand on Dad's shoulder, said, "Drums are universal to most every culture, like water and circles. The drumming sure is hypnotic, isn't it?"

It *was* hypnotic, and Roberto was one of the drummer men. A group of them came around the side of the building, chanting the same melody over and over, verse after verse, in words we couldn't understand.

Passing us, Roberto nodded his head to our family and called out, "Rita's and my house for lunch, as usual."

"Why, thank you!" Mom called back, raising a Tupperware cake holder. They loved her traditional pineapple-coconut cake every Christmas.

And then Roberto caught my eye. Something passed from him to me, something deeply spiritual and a little scary. At that instant, I felt an irresistible summons and found myself walking toward the line of drummers, hopping from foot to foot in rhythm with the Jemez dancing girls.

Mom grabbed my coat sleeve. "Not for Anglos," she whispered. She pulled me back gently, but I stumbled and fell in the dirt, swallowing grit. I was so embarrassed, so sure everyone's eyes were on me. Choking back tears, I struggled to my feet and ran to our van, which was locked, and crawled up onto the front fender for a good cry.

The drumming faded into the distance, and in a few minutes the crowd scattered, and my family came to walk me up to Roberto's for lunch.

"Feeling better, honey?" Mom asked.

I nodded and locked my lips shut until they were dry and chapped.

There must have been fifty people packed into Rita and Roberto's tiny pueblo house, so no one noticed how quiet I was. We all dug into the mountain of cheese enchiladas, sopped up red chile with Indian flat bread, and washed it all down with warm Coke. Roberto was so lively that day, so *alive*, carrying little Lupita around on his shoulders, laughing and telling jokes and praising Rita's cooking.

Thinking about that day while I perched high up in the oak tree, I sorely missed the person Roberto had been just a month earlier. He'd left so many loving people behind, so much undone. Was that why it seemed he was trying to reach me, to tell me something he wanted me to pass on to Rita and his children and especially to Lupita? But why me?

I parted the leaves for a quick glance down, and gasped at how far I was from the ground. My thoughts slid back to Roberto, the day he tumbled from that roof and his broken body in the bed of the truck. Suddenly I panicked, chose strong branches to scramble down until I was close enough to jump to the ground. In one piece.

Chapter Fourteen
Daphne

Truth is, after my Molly and Alice went to heaven—and who knows where Miss Amelia ended up?—some folks down in the quarters started whispering that maybe it wasn't me did it. Maybe it was Eulie witching those Nethercotts dead out of pure jealousy. I'm thinking she knows she did it her own self, and now she's scared that Lila and Sal are just primed to find out the truth. But what if I don't like what they find out? Twists my brain guessing, is it better to know for sure you killed some folks, or just keep believing you didn't, or wondering forever if you might could of?

What I do know for sure is that there's something special about those two girls, Sal and Lila, and something big about this day that's not like any other one.

Maybe that's why Eulie's back after so long, scared witless and cat-walking around this place.

She was a mean one, back in those long-ago days. One time I made just the prettiest pineapple upside-down cake, the kind you bake in a skillet floating in butter and sugar 'til it gets all syrupy in the bottom of the pan. I flipped it over onto one of Miss Amelia's china platters, beaming with pride. Well, you know what Père Jacques would say about pride, how it comes before a fall. Eulie made the fall her own self. Looked me right in the eye as she acted like the platter slid out of her hand, and she let out a blood-chilling yelp that brought Miss Amelia running into the kitcken just as Eulie ducked out the back door. There it was, the whole sticky brown-sugary mess splattered all over the walls, and Miss Amelia's fancy Yankee plate smashed to bits. She was so mad that her face turned red, and she shoved me outside the door 'til I fell with my face in the dirt of Luke's flower bed, and she made me stay out there all night, even when lightning came. Luke covered me over with a burlap sack, but he was careful to take it off next morning before Miss Amelia came out to see if I'd been fried up by a bolt of lightning. Eulie was right behind her, gloating. Ooh, I hated that girl, I did.

But I was never mean enough to do to her what she did to me. So, when she made me crazy prancing around telling everybody how light and airy her buckwheat griddle cakes were, and how the tomatoes were bigger and sweeter now that she was tending to the garden, which she wasn't, 'cause Luke Mullin was, I'd wait 'til she sliced up a bunch of tomatoes on a plate for the Judge's dinner. Then, when Eulie turned her head, I'd drop a wiggle-worm from Luke Mullin's compost heap under a lettuce leaf before she could put that plate in front of the Judge. Stand by and watch for him to spot that worm crawling in and out of the tomato seeds. Come to think of it, that got me even up with Eulie and the Judge, both!

Sometimes I caught Eulie and Miss Amelia talking at the top of the stairs, and Lord knows *what* they were scheming. You ask me, and I'd say Miss Amelia favored Eulie because she was saggy and ugly, and the Judge never gave her a glance. Some ways, I guess Eulie was lucky, because the Judge's eyes were all the time finding me, and his sneaky looks chilled me like I'd poked my toe into the River Styx, floating toward hell like Tante Drucilla always told the story.

So, anyway, Miss Amelia had Eulie to cleaning her own private room upstairs, dusting all those perfume bottles and tucking the sheets tight as a drum, like I used to do. I prayed Eulie wouldn't go snooping under the bed for the box where the *bébés* were. Wasn't any of her business.

She thought everything in the house was her business, though, including Alice and Molly, but they didn't like her even a little.

Alice said, "Why, she's purely awful, Daphne. I reckon a smile would crack her mean old face clear in two."

Molly just said, "I pretend she's not here. I make her disappear."

My girls, I tell you!

Working side by side with Eulie was vexing. I admit it: a time or two when she turned her back, I spit into the soup in her kettle, or switched out the sugar for salt when she was fixing to make one of her apple pandowdy puddings Miss Amelia raved on about. Birdie tolerated her, but me, some days I just had to get out of the kitchen for fear I'd scratch Eulie's fleshy gray face right off its bones.

Chapter Fifteen
Daphne

One day Birdie and I were out by Luke Mullin's garden hanging a wash. I said, "Birdie, you figure I can ever learn the conjure art? Do some magic? Get to be as good as you at it?"

"Better be good at it, child, 'cause you ain't much with a needle and thread, that's for sure, and your pie crust could just about brick up a well." Birdie chuckled. Sounded like a cackling hen.

I must have been about thirteen then, before the Judge took up with me. Birdie wrung out a bedsheet. I mean, she could squeeze every drop out until that thing was nearly dry as paper. I'd seen her wring the neck of a chicken same way. An hour later, it was fried up crisp on the Judge's plate.

Birdie whispered so Luke Mullin couldn't hear. Never could tell if he was listening even if his head was pointed right at you, because the man's eyes were crossed worse than the XX's *mon cher* Isaac used to sign his name. Isaac could read about as good as Molly, but he couldn't write yet, and anyway, the Judge didn't know Isaac read words, which is how it had to stay for the sake of his back.

So, Birdie leaned into me behind a sheet flapping in the breeze. Said, "Some of the mojo art you gotta get from the sap that runs in a child's mother, and your mama Henriette, bless and rest her soul, she wasn't no conjure woman." Birdie stepped back and looked at my whole self good and hard. "I remember the hour you was born, child. Born with a caul over your face, like a widow's veil. That's a sign you born with the power. It's running through you somewheres. Just got to learn how to leech it out."

"Can you teach me, Birdie?"

Long pause. "Maybe." She snapped a wet sheet smooth. "It ain't all for the good, you know. Ain't no game to play."

"I know, Birdie, but I just want a small passel of it. Can you show me how to charm Isaac into being a lovesick hound?" I asked.

"Oh, child, too late for that. He's already barking! Now, hush about that, 'cause I s'pect Luke Mullin over there is just a little sweet on you, too."

"Birdie!" I squoze myself into cross-eyes, and Birdie slapped my derrière with a wet towel.

"Watch you don't freeze that way, child."

Birdie was sure like a *maman* to me, and I was needing one, living apart from the *tantes*, and ever since Henriette left me, she hadn't come back even once. She must be haunting some other planatation, I tell you true, maybe where my daddy Ventoure lived out his days.

So, Birdie taught me a thing or two, like a *maman* would of, maybe better. One night I helped her undo a curse down in the quarters. "Listen careful. This healing tea, it's made from a frizzy chicken's gizzard lining," she told me, holding up a foul-smelling brew. "Boil that gizzard in water that you already boiled silver in for a good long while. That potion gonna cure a whammy in the blink of an eye. If it don't kill you first."

Couldn't spend all my time with Birdie, back then. Miss Amelia had me looking after Alice and Molly a good part of it, but that's all right, because I loved those pretty little girls with all my heart. Together they added up to my age. Oh, yes, I knew numbers. Couldn't read, but numbers are easy. All you got to do is count your fingers and toes, and if you run out, you can throw in your elbows and nose and, well, I s'pose boys got one more part to count than girls.

Alice and Molly were sweet-tempered girls, but I pitied how they had to be dressed up all the time in fancy frocks, not s'posed to get dirty, and ribbons tied in bows in their hair all the long day. You know what they loved? They loved going down to the quarters and playing with our barefoot, ragged little ones down there, under the watch of the old *tantes* while the daddies and *mamans* sweated all back-bent out in the fields.

Molly and Alice, they played toss-the-ring, and run-and-hide. Played with rag-doll babies Tante Drucilla sewed up—black babies with snarly hair and peppercorn eyes and smeary red smiles. Up at the big house, the girls had porcelain dolls with little red apple circles painted on cheeks as white as cream. Those stiff dolls didn't do a thing but sit there looking pretty, not even a smile on their faces. So, you know how it goes. My girls, my Molly and Alice, snuck down to the quarters every chance they got. Molly used to say, "You know what I love best of all in the world, Daphne? Running down to where your people live and getting filthy dirty playing."

Sometimes Miss Amelia came down there to spread a little cheer, passing out parcels of Birdie's maple fudge on the Fourth of July, and a coin for each of the children. Nothing to spend it on, of course, but they'd hold on to that piece of money, and in the winter when the Judge gave us shoes, they'd drop that coin into their shoe, and the lump in the shoe made them feel rich.

So, Tante Drucilla told me that Miss Amelia was down there one day, and spied Alice and Molly, one of them tossing a tight ball of wool yarn at Eulie's Tom, and the other jumping on poor Tom's back so he couldn't hit the ball with the rotten-wood plank fixed over his shoulder.

That was the last time Alice and Molly went down to the quarters to play.

———

That Lila, I know she caught sight of me standing at the table the awful night my girls died. I would of given Lila a cupful of the sweet-tart raspberries if I could of.

Ever since that terrible night, folks have said it's me who poisoned those sweet girls. Honest truth is, I don't know what *did* happen, what with the confusion and that mess of a gâteau and all. Eulie and me both had a hand in baking the cake, and it sat on the windowsill cooling, so anybody could of sprinkled something mean and bad over it, just dried up oleander leaves or a drop or two of its sap, and why they'd do it, I don't know.

I just know I was there, running back and forth from the dining room to the kitchen three times to every one of Eulie's, like I always did. Didn't matter to anybody that I was sweating like a dog while the family was working their way through the first course and the second, and I was cranking that big old fan to keep the Judge and Miss Amelia and my girls cool as could be.

Oh, I do miss those girls, more than I miss having skin-and-bones of my own. I'd about swear that I spot them sometimes up on the back roof, sitting up there watching the pond out beyond the house, or else jumping on Molly's bed. Or maybe I'm just wishing I could see them and hoping they forgive me for whatever happened that night on Molly's birthday. Lord, I can't forgive my own self; how could they?

Chapter Sixteen

Lila

I was barely out of the tree when Gabe came bounding around the house breathless, as though he'd been running a marathon. He crumbled onto the damp grass under my giant oak, wiping sweat with his sleeve.

"Guess what I saw out there."

"I don't know, what?"

"Nothing. Well, just an empty shack." There was some hesitation in his voice.

"But?"

"It's kind of strange the way it's plopped down there in the middle of an overgrown field. I just about needed a scythe to cut my way through the bramble getting there. Not even a path leading to the shack. Then suddenly there's a flat, cleared circle all around the little house. Looks like nobody's been there in years."

"I saw a light burning last night. It had to be coming from there."

"You'd think. But there are no signs of life, like the place was abandoned a century ago. And it probably doesn't have electricity, anyway."

"So, why's the brush cleared?" I asked.

"Beats me."

"I gotta see this, show me." I jumped to my feet, and we started back across the field. Hot as it was, I still wished I'd worn a sweatshirt and jeans, because my arms and legs were getting scratched up by the prickly bushes. Gabe did his best to clear them away for me. They snapped back as soon as we passed. Halfway to the cottage, I looked back, and the brush was so dense that I couldn't see the ground floor of the mansion. For a second I panicked. There were *snakes* in Louisiana! They could be anywhere in this thick growth. I listened for hissing, and finally we came to the clearing. A wide swath of scorched grass encircled the cottage, as if one of those movie spaceships had landed there. The cottage itself was just an ancient shack, with a patched roof slanting toward the ground.

We snuck a peek in the small square of a window. No curtains, no shades. There was a guy inside, sitting spine-straight in the rocking chair with his back to us. I jumped away from the window.

"He must have come back. He's in there, Gabe."

"Who? Where? I don't see anyone."

"Yes you do! You're just being stubborn."

"Am not. There's no one there, Lila, zip, zero, nada, nothing."

A pot bubbled away on the stove, steam rising and fogging the window a little. How could Gabe *not* see these things? "You at least see the steam on the window, don't you?"

"Lila, there's no window. Just an open square where a window used to be."

"Maybe you're not supposed to see it, just me," I said, feeling the color drain from my face. "He's there, plain as day, a black man wearing a plaid shirt and overalls. There's a floppy white hat hooked over the back of the chair. I've seen him twice before, Gabe. His name's Luke. Sal told me. He rakes leaves in front of the house, just keeps raking and raking, even at night, and then when I blink, he's gone."

"Not another one," Gabe groaned, shaking his head.

"Look again," I said miserably.

He tried. "Okay, here's exactly what I see. A rocking chair with its back to us. Yeah, I see the hat hooked over the back. I suppose it could almost look like a head, if you squint and look at it through the slits of your eyes."

"No, that's not it! Clear as anything, the man's reading a book that he's holding out at arm's distance, like Dad does, like he's farsighted and needs glasses. Look at his feet. See the little white dog curled there?" The hair on my arms and neck stood up. I tapped on the door, not wanting to scare the man. He didn't move or shout *come on in*, and the dog still lay there with a paw on the man's foot.

"Must be deaf," I said.

"Right, and the dog, too."

"I don't care if you believe me or not." I pounded on the door. Any harder and I'd have put my fist through the flinty wood. No response. "I've got to go inside." Swallowing a hard glob of fear in my throat, I pressed the old-fashioned door latch and heard it click open. "Hello? Mind if we come in?" My voice wobbled. I peeked around the door.

Nobody there! The rocking chair was in the same spot, and a straw mattress on the floor, against the wall. No man, no dog. Nothing boiling. I touched the stove; cold.

A pair of cracked, lace-up boots stood right in front of the bed, like somebody'd just stepped out of them. Gardening tools—a hoe and a rake and a shovel—leaned in a corner, with a pair of mud-crusted gloves across them.

I dug my nails into Gabe's arm. "It's all gone—the man in the plaid shirt, the dog, the bubbling pot. All gone."

Gabe blew hair off his forehead, which was furled in lines of puzzlement and fear that mirrored my own. Or was it worry? He grabbed me by the shoulders and shook me, as if he could shake the vision out of my mind.

He yelled, "Lila, listen to me, *listen!* There's no one there, and there never was anything there besides an old abandoned shack and a few pieces of rickety furniture and some clothes and tools. No man, no dog. Say it with me: NO ONE THERE!"

I yanked myself away from his grip. "I know what I saw, Gabe."

He pulled me down beside him on the little wooden

step leading to the shack. "Okay, say you saw it, saw a man and a boiling pot and a dog. How do I put this?" He wrinkled his brow, thinking it through, while I reviewed every detail, to etch it all in my memory.

"Okay, okay, let's figure out how Camilla rigged this one so you'd see him, and a flash of a second later, I wouldn't. Think about it, Lila. She'd have to have a full hocus-pocus staff of prop men and bit actors wherever we happened to be every minute, day or night. But do we ever see anyone dashing around the plantation? Do we ever see *anyone* besides Camilla and Sal?"

"And Sal's at school," I said slowly.

"We're not talking about a simple thing like piano keys or a plant sliding across the piano. We're talking some complex Disney quality staging here. Think about it," he said again.

It hit me, then, like a fist to my belly: "You don't even believe it's rigged anymore, do you, Gabe? You think every bit of it's in my head—Roberto and Daphne and the raking man. I'm a psycho, that's what you think!"

He didn't deny it.

I stood up, reeling with dizzy fear and felt my eyes swim in my head. I was so sure of it all, a minute ago. And now?

"Omigod, Gabe, what's happening to me? What's *happening* to me?"

Chapter Seventeen
Daphne

We went rooting, Birdie and me, but sure as anything not picking oleander. Every chance Birdie got, she warned me to keep away from that deadly stuff. "Jest a lick of the sap gonna make you retch up your whole dinner," she reminded me.

So, we walked out to the wild field beyond Luke Mullin's house-garden to fill our aprons like cotton-picking bags with roots and herbs and leaves. Birdie used every one of them for doctoring, some boiled in a tea for miserable head colds, and some ground up and smeared with lard on a stinging sore place, like maybe the back of a man who's been under the whip.

"Lookit here." She showed me a clump of tall yellow things, about the meanest-looking flower I ever saw. "Flannel mullein," she said with a deep sigh of contentment. "Best thing out here, that's for sure. Good for the stomach, for when you can't catch your breath, or when you got the achy tooth—just about anything you can name."

"Can it make you rich?"

"Can't do that, child, but sure can keep your feets warm. Catch ahold of one of them big ole leaves. Go on, feel of it."

I did, and it felt thick and sinewy.

"See? Come winter, line your shoes with 'em, and you be a lot more comftable."

Birdie showed me ganderroot and bitterroot; asafetida, which smelled like garlic, if you ask me; catnip and dogbane; sweetgum and gumweed; sneezeweed and ragweed and rattleweed. And then there were the worts, lots of different ones. Tell you the truth, every one of them looked just alike to me.

"Pitiful, that's what you is." Birdie snatched the broken and smashed roots out of my apron bag and dumped them in the field. I about felt an inch tall, watching her stooped over, rooting around with her back to me and quieter than a sparrow.

Finally, walking back to the house, she fingered that clear stone she always kept in her apron pocket. Said, "I see roots ain't gonna do it. You gonna learn about manure, first chance I get."

Well, that didn't sound too savory to me, but I stayed quiet.

The chance came quicker than we expected. Oncle Joe, Therese's father, drove a nail into his thumb trying to fix up Therese and Shem's cabin. Pulled it out himself, but it left a serious big hole spouting blood. I watched Birdie hurry to fix Oncle Joe a poultice of cow manure from the pasture, a piece of spiderweb hanging off the second-floor eaves, soot from the Judge's fireplace, and some good old hog lard she kept by in the kitchen. I mixed them all together in a tin cup, like she showed me, holding my nose against the awful smell, and I toted it down to Oncle Joe's. He was whimpering real shallow. Me, I'd of been howling like I did with my ear. My head was still pretty raw and looked as ugly as that mullein flower, which is why I took to wearing the hat slung over where my ear used to be.

So, Birdie smeared that concoction over Oncle Joe's thumb, but not before I got a good long look at that terrible sight. She wrapped it up in red flannel rags, tore off a strip to tie it loose, and gave him some laudanum tea to put him to sleep 'til the pain eased down.

After Oncle Joe, Birdie said, "Lord be, child, you is shaking like a leaf."

"I don't think I'm made for this healing, Birdie."

"Uh-huh."

Hurt me that she agreed. I hoped she'd say, "Why sure you is! Just take time, that's all, child." But she didn't say another word until we got back home, and then she said, "Conjure doctoring ain't what you're meant for, but I know you got the sap running through you down deep. I been

thinking hard on it. What you is called to, Daphne, is, you
is meant to be a tree talker."

"I don't know what you mean, Birdie, tree talker."

"Poor child, your mama didn't live long enough to tell
you about Aferca, she being one of the Wolof people." She
went on to make up for poor dead Henriette. Told me Africans say that everything has a spirit, not just people. Rocks
do, and mountains, and dogs and cats and snakes, and
water and wind, and especially trees. Birdie said some
people can talk to the spirits plain and simple. Just got to
learn how to do it.

"Tree talking run in families," Birdie said. "I heard
Henriette one time say that your daddy had the know-how
back in Aferca, and I s'pect he passed it to you, child."

"You telling me, Birdie, that I can plunk myself down
under a tree and have a talking-to like you and I are
doing?"

"Not immediate. Got to take time to get to know your
tree, make friends, listen good before you say a word to it.
That tree knows good from evil, and it'll tell you, if you
ask it just the right way."

"Sounds crazy, Birdie, truly, but if my daddy . . . well,
I s'pose I could give it a try." Not much chance of it, I was
thinking, but it was the only thing I had left over from my
daddy. Got to take what you can get in this life.

"First thing before breakfast tomorrow, we gonna pick
you out your tree, and you gonna learn to talk with it like
it's your best friend. Be thinking of which one's your tree."

She blew out the candle and left me stretched out on
my straw mattress behind the stove. I didn't know whether

she was mad with me 'cause I was hopeless at doctoring, or whether she had a sparky new hope that I'd learn some little piece of the mojo art, if talking to trees was *it*.

That's what I decided to believe, by myself there in the dark for my few minutes of peace before anyone came for me: that I could learn to be a tree talker like my daddy and make Birdie proud of me.

I didn't know that a tree's rough bark would be the last thing I'd feel against my skin, my heel thumping against it, thumping against it. Or that its earthy spice would be what I'd smell those last few minutes while I could still breathe air.

Chapter Eighteen

Lila

Gabe and I sat on the front step of the shack for a while, silent in our own thoughts, until I pulled myself together.

Walking back to the mansion, he said, "We've gotta tell Mom and Dad about this *thing* you're going through."

"No! At least not yet. They'll go bonkers and rip us right out of this place. I need some answers first, Gabe. Please?"

He paused. I could see him weighing it all in his mind. "You think Sal might help clear some of this up? Maybe tell us what Camilla has up her sleeve, or whatever?"

Just grasping. He didn't sound at all convinced, but I

said, "Sure, we'll check it out with Sal. She'd be honest with me." I didn't add how she'd told me that the raking man, the one she'd called Luke, was a ghost, as if there was absolutely nothing strange about that fact.

Gabe said, "I don't like it, but okay, just until tonight, and then we lay it on Mom and Dad, 'cause this is too big for me to handle alone."

"Shh, don't say anything, there's Dad's car coming up the driveway."

"Soft-shell crab po-boys!" Dad called out, flashing a big bag of lunch. "Piled to the sky, on crusty French rolls. A Louisiana speciality. And beignets for dessert. New Orleans is famous for them, but these from New Roads aren't a bad substitute."

We set out our picnic on one of the wrought-iron tables at the back of the house. I kept flashing Gabe *don't say a word* looks, and he nodded in agreement.

Dad said, "After lunch I'll take off for Baton Rouge to investigate a Creole jambalaya place along the way, and a Cajun grocery for my magazine article, then pick up Mom. We'll try to get back before that storm hits. You kids have enough to keep you going around here?"

"Yeah," I assured him. "We brought checkers and Pictionary." As if we had nothing better to do.

Gabe said, "And if we get bored, we can always interview the Laurel Oaks head chef ghost for you."

I kicked him under the table.

Dad frowned. "I don't want to hear about the ghost stuff, kids. Remember, it's all for show around here. That's how they keep these places filled with customers." We all looked around at the darkened house, the empty parking lot. "Except this week, I guess," Dad added with a grin.

"Agreed, no ghost stuff." Gabe put his hand up in the Boy Scout pledge, and I crossed my heart, but I did *not* hope to die.

By the time we scarfed down the lighter-than-air beignets, we were covered with powdered sugar, so of course Gabe had to take another shower. And then it was practice time. I swear, ghosts could be oozing out of the pipes and walking through walls, but Gabe *had* to practice his trombone an hour a day for his solo in the school jazz band concert.

Dad took off for Baton Rouge. So, I holed up alone in the Maude Eberly room, trying to ignore the funky toots of Gabe's horn across the hall while I waited impatiently for Sal to get home. I had a zillion questions for her.

The useless A/C was on full blast and still I felt hot and sticky with powdered sugar, like one large glazed donut. I opened my door. The black cat strutted in and jumped on my bed. My luck, she'd probably drop a litter of kittens on my pillow. But she was company, better than nothing. Man, was I feeling sorry for myself. And scared. What if I *was* going crazy?

I paced the room; the cat's eyes followed me lazily, but when I stood in front of that Fragrant Rose wall hanging, she got up on all fours and hunched her back into a U.

"What, you don't like needlepoint?" I asked. I brought the sampler over to the cat, who jumped to the floor and scurried under the bed. I turned the sampler around to look at it more closely. Didn't see anything that would send a cat spinning out of orbit, but just to be contrary, I got down on the floor and shoved the frame under the bed. The cat ran out the other side of the bed and took a flying leap onto the coatrack, clinging to those antlers with her life. I hung the sampler back on the wall. Couldn't get it to hang straight, but at least the cat came down, with her teeth bared and her yellow eyes glaring hatred.

I opened the door and shooed her out into the hall, then sank into the love seat, trying to figure out what Daphne meant when she said, *Find the babies, the babies in the wall.*

The wall hanging; the babies in the wall. Was there a connection? A closer look at the sampler told me nothing. Too many unanswered questions. Fresh air, that's what I needed to clear my head.

I thundered down the stairs and outside, galloping around the perimeter of the house. Passing the corner between the General Store and the house, the corner where Daphne'd been photographed, I took another lap around until I started to calm down. The shade of that giant oak looked inviting. I dropped down in its shelter, in a pile of leaves. Leaves Luke had raked? My thoughts would *not* compute.

At the sound of grinding brakes, I looked up to see Sal jumping down the school bus steps. She skipped up the long driveway, munching a red apple.

"Sal!"

She seemed startled. Tenting her eyes, she spotted me.

"It's Thursday. How come you don't have to go to school?" she asked, dropping down beside me.

"My parents got us excused for three days for this trip."

"I s'pose you can do that if you're the kind goes to school regular." She offered me a bite of the apple. "Left over from my lunch. Miss Camilla packs me lunch enough for a army." Her words were mooshy with apple. "You picked the right tree. It ain't jealous about giving its shade. This is Daphne's tree, all right."

A strange feeling rippled through my skin. Sal watched me shiver and said, "I expect you're wondering about stuff."

"A million things."

"Fire away."

"I don't know where to start, so I'll just ask, who's here exactly?"

"Just me and Miss Camilla."

"No, the *others*."

"From the spirit world? Depends who you ask. The girls, Molly and Alice, that's what their mama called them, some folks see them sitting there on the roof watching, just banging their pretty shoes on the house. If I ever saw 'em, I'm sure they wouldn't talk to me, because that's the way they was brought up, or as *up* as they got before they passed."

I looked over at the roof; didn't see anyone. "Who else?"

"Well, you ran into a couple yourself. Old Luke, for one, but like I said, I don't ever see him, either."

"Can't, or don't?"

She tossed the apple core into the bushes. "What's the

difference? Mostly the ones I spot are the ladies, hissing at each other like mad cats. They are *restless* spirits, those two."

"Two?" I asked, starting to tremble.

"Eulie, one, and Daphne, two. Don't they teach you to count over at your school?"

"Yes, but not to count dead people."

"They ain't dead," Sal said with a shrug. "They just in the next place folks go. That's what my grandmama tells. She comes over here, times. Once she pointed to some-body I never saw before and said, 'That gal's name is Eu-lie. I believe she's totin' a load of guilt on her scrawny shoulders, and it's making her mad and bad.'"

"What's she feeling guilty about?" I asked.

Sal shrugged. "Ask my grandmama. Woo-wee! It's thick as molasses out here."

She thrust her palm out, and a few drops splattered on it. "Looks like we're in for a rainy time."

"Why's the one you call Eulie guilty?" I demanded.

"I didn't say she *was* guilty. My grandmama said she *might* be dragging some guilty feeling around. Different. Might could have to do with poisoning those little white girls up on the roof."

"I knew it! Daphne didn't do it at all!"

"Did I say that?" She cupped her ear to the tree and asked, "Did you hear that, trunk? Didn't think so!"

Sal jumped up, dancing and twirling as the rain began coming down. The harder the rain fell, the faster Sal twirled until I was dizzy just watching her.

Big, punishing drops pelted me, slapped my skin, and in seconds my clothes were soaked. "Let's run for cover up on the porch, or under that thick Spanish moss until the storm passes."

"Nah, I'm wash 'n' wear," Sal said, opening her arms to the rain.

Suddenly I felt rooted with the tree, the one Sal had called Daphne's tree. The wind picked up, lashing its leaves and my hair. My shirt whipped around my waist. Rain slapped my bare belly.

"You okay, Yankee girl?" Sal shouted.

I couldn't even answer, stunned and fascinated by the violence of the sudden storm that battered us. The head of a statue toppled from its shoulders and smashed into shards inches away. Two porch chairs split apart, boards and splinters banging against the windows and doors like they were begging for shelter. Whole limbs blew off younger trees nearby, but Daphne's tree stood braced against the wind. And right out there under the open sky, Sal stopped spinning and planted her feet wide as though she could catch the rain in the barrel of her arms.

Lightning split the sky.

"Sal!" I shouted through the thunder rumbling loud as a freight train. "We better run into the house. We're lightning rods out here!"

Sal wrapped her arms and legs around Daphne's tree and clung to it like a koala bear as a clap of thunder shook the ground beneath my feet. "Best place to be, right here," she protested. "Grab hold."

I locked my arms around a sturdy low branch of Daphne's tree.

And then I heard a quiet, insistent voice: *Safe with me.*

I jumped.

The Africans say it's God rolling stones in heaven.

The voice was a deep, rumbling male voice, unlike any I'd ever heard before. I looked around wildly. No one there, just Sal and me.

Chapter Nineteen
Daphne

Birdie said, "Pick careful, child. Don't just latch to any old tree."

We walked all round the yard, her muttering low to herself each time I'd put my hand to a tree she knew was the wrong one.

"Birdie, I feel like a fool patting and pounding tree trunks."

"Trust, child. The spirit of the tree gonna let you know, sure."

"I just don't get that, Birdie, trees and rocks having spirits like people."

She bristled, like I'd just insulted her man Nathan. "Why you think they got Holy Water outside the church and you Catholic folks touch it here and there to you? Why you think Luke Mullin plant sweet basil both sides of the front door?"

"That one's easy. For good luck, to keep the bad spirits out, same as horseshoes over the door. Everybody knows that."

"Um-hmn. And what brings the good luck if'n it's not the spirit in that water, in that sweet basil or them horseshoes? Think, child. Nothing special about a frizzy chicken's gizzard lining 'cept it cures a bad whammy, and why? 'Cause of the spirit residing in it. Simple as that."

So I kept patting and pounding and petting those trees like they were house hounds. Came to an oak tree out front that wasn't any bigger round than a tea saucer, and Birdie stopped in front of it. I saw the hairs stand up at her neck.

"That my tree, you reckon?"

"Not my place to say," she mumbled, "but something coming off it, you feel it?"

I laid the pink of my hand flat against the smooth trunk. The thing wasn't old enough to be chipping crusty bark yet, but I swear, it *hummed* at my hand, and I liked to never pull away. "Well, shut my mouth wide open!" I cried. "I do believe this is my tree."

"Um-hmn," Birdie agreed.

"It's buzzing at me."

"Tree's spirit's talking." And she walked away, leaving me scared and real excited, alone with the tree.

It wasn't any impressive tree, barely taller than Isaac, with a nice umbrella of foresty-green leaves. I listened to them flurrying in the breeze, 'til I swear I could hear some of them distinctive. It was like at church, everybody singing, *"Le Père, le Fils, et le Saint-Esprit . . ."* and it sounded like one big thrumming melody, but if you listened close, you could pick out this voice and that, separate from the whole bunch of them.

I listened every chance I got away from the house, 'til one day I heard sap running inside that trunk. But the tree sure didn't talk to me, though I listened and whispered to it quiet, so Luke Mullin wouldn't hear.

Thing is, Luke Mullin could creep up on you and be there a long time before you noticed him, and you'd wonder, what did I say that I didn't want him to hear? Then you'd turn to him to say, "Good day for planting?" and he'd take off faster than the crack of a whip.

He's a slippery one, maybe because he was a free man all his life in the other world and doesn't want to get himself caught in this one. Or maybe because he's holding some secret close that he's not about to let loose of. Or he's an angel, watching out for somebody. Not me. He's sure shut himself off from me, and won't talk to Sal either, but I don't know why.

Important thing is, Lila's found my tree. Sal saw to it. But Lila doesn't know yet why it's *my* tree.

Chapter Twenty

Lila

"Storm be over soon," Sal said. "Look there."

A dark-skinned woman ran out of the house, wielding an ax. Her old-fashioned dress and white petticoat whirled around her in the wind. Still clinging to the branch, I wiped rain out of my eyes with my shoulder to get a clearer view. Not a woman; a girl. A girl in a yellow turban. Daphne! She ran down the stairs, ax raised over her head.

"Hoo! I guess the storm was fierce enough to scare someone on the Other Side," Sal said. "I'm thinking Eulie made that storm brew up."

I had to shout over the raging storm. "You mentioned her before. Who's Eulie, exactly?"

"Best I can figure out, she used to be a kitchen girl here, back a whole long time ago. Just like her to call up a fierce storm. But somebody else means to stop it cold. Could be Daphne. Look at her," Sal said, snickering. "Look like she's chopping at the ground to hack up a cobra."

"What *is* she doing with the ax?" I shouted.

The answer didn't come from Sal, but from that other voice, that mellow male voice I'd heard a few minutes ago: *She's cutting the storm in two . . . splitting the clouds. It's what the Africans used to do to tame a storm.*

And then, as quickly as it had come on, the raging stopped, the sky brightened, the leaves settled peacefully on their branches. The only sign of the storm now was the gentle *plink-plink* of raindrops off the oak leaves and weeping willows.

Her job done, the girl—Daphne?—disappeared, just as she had the night before.

Sal shook all over like a dog coming in out of the rain.

I felt pummeled, beaten, cold as ice, but I had to ask. "Who was that talking about splitting clouds and God rolling stones?"

Sal shrugged. "I didn't hear nobody. Who you think?"

"I don't know what to think. There's nobody else around here but you and me and—I guess you'd count Daphne up on that porch, but that couldn't have been her voice. Old Luke?" I asked.

Sal tilted her head from side to side. "Doubt it. Folks

say he don't talk a'tall." She patted the tree, pulling away a palm full of wet bark. "Coulda been him."

"Sal! Trees do *not* talk."

"This one do, if you know how to listen. My grandmama told me about folks who're tree talkers. I ain't one, but could be you are and don't even know it." She giggled. "Wouldn't that be a kick?"

"I absolutely do not talk to trees," I said.

"Don't stop him from talking to you, though. My grandmama, she says every tree's got a name. I s'pose Daphne had a name for this one, and once you got a name for a thing, it's yours. This one sure ain't mine."

I put my ear to the tree, listening to—nothing. I must have imagined that calm, reassuring voice. Suddenly I felt ridiculous even thinking I'd heard him, *it*, speak. "I'm freezing, I've got to get out of these wet clothes."

Sal said, "Miss Camilla gonna have my tail feathers for soaking up this outfit she bought me special for the school picture today."

"Come upstairs. I'll give you something to put on while your clothes dry, and Camilla will never know the difference."

We dripped all the way up the stairs and threw our clothes over the bathtub. No sound from Gabe's room. He must have fallen asleep after trombone practice.

My T-shirt hung down to Sal's knees. In my room, she curled into a ball on the rug in front of the hearth while I got a fire started. Who expected to use the fireplace in the heat of Louisiana's October? But the sudden intense storm

Eulie had brought on chilled me to my bones, and the heat and crackling flames were cozy.

What was I *thinking?* Eulie hadn't caused the storm. The biker couple had warned us that a late-afternoon storm was coming. A ghost cannot start a storm, I reminded myself.

Daphne had stopped it, though. I'd seen it happen.

The silent, cold shadow-fire flickered and billowed on the walls, like a ghostly dance, and I felt chilled all over again. Sal looked weird backlit by the fire, and for a second I wondered if she was a ghost herself.

No! She went to school, ate apples, clung to that tree. She was as solid as me. Human. Alive. Maybe I *was* going nuts, like Gabe thought.

I hunched on the floor in front of the fire. My stomach growled. Why weren't Mom and Dad back?

It's God rolling stones in heaven. The mysterious voice resounded in my head. The room was bathed in shadows lengthened by the eerie glow of the fire. A spook scene if I ever saw one. I rubbed my hands; the sandpaper sound unnerved me. Like, I wasn't unhinged already?

I scooted around just to let the fire bake my shoulders, I told myself, but the truth was, that sampler on the wall . . . *Fragrant the rose is* . . . was really creeping me out. I had to turn my back on it, like the cat did. And where *was* the cat?

The phone jangled, jarring us out of our daydreams. And at the same time, there was Gabe pounding on my door. Sal let him in while I flipped the phone open. Dad's strained voice filled my head.

"Honey, let me tell you first of all that we're okay."

I gripped the phone tight, motioning for Gabe to come closer. "What's the not-okay part, Dad?"

Gabe tossed his hair back. "What? WHAT?"

"Shh!" I pressed the phone closer to catch every word, holding my breath.

"We had a little accident with the car, honey."

"An accident? Omigod, are you hurt? Is Mom?" I bit my finger until it throbbed, bracing for the worst.

"Nothing serious. Thank God traffic was moving so slowly. Less impact, but enough. I have a couple of cracked ribs from hitting the steering wheel. Also a slight whiplash."

"What about Mom?" Hesitation. "Dad! What about Mom?"

"She's doing fine but . . ." The *but* silently bounced off the walls of the room. "She took a blow to her head on the dashboard. She has a slight concussion, and they want to keep her here overnight. Both of us, for observation. Have you got something to write down the hospital number?"

I pantomimed pen-and-paper, which Gabe snatched out of my backpack.

"We need to stay here until they know for sure what's going on. You two will be okay tonight?"

"No problem," I reassured Dad. No problem. Just a violent storm, a vanishing gardener, a talking tree, a neurotic cat, and one New Mexico girl who was possibly crazy as a loon, seeing things, hearing voices. We were buried in problems.

"It was the oddest thing, honey. There wasn't a drop of

water on the road, but I swear this VW two cars ahead of us slid as though it was hydroplaning and spun around until it was an unavoidable target for the Buick following it. I swerved to avoid rear-ending the Buick. Smashed into a guardrail. It was a freak accident, unexplainable. And after that, rain started pouring down like mad, out of no-where."

"Don't forget those bikers. They said the weatherman predicted rain."

"Yes, but so sudden, and then stopping in a flash? I've never seen anything like it. I guess we're just a little skit-tish. After all, we're in hurricane country. Is Gabe there, honey?"

Parents aren't supposed to be in accidents. They're supposed to be the ones taking care of us. And then I real-ized how selfish and little-girlish this thought was. With a shaky hand I passed the phone to Gabe, silently remind-ing myself, *Mom and Dad are alive; they're okay.*

"Jeez," Gabe said soberly. Maybe he was getting the real story, something Dad wanted to protect me from.

"What's going on?" I cried.

He waved me off. "Okay, buzz us in the morning or if anything changes."

He handed me the phone, and I heard the warning in Dad's voice now. "We'll be back as early as possible tomor-row. Get something to eat at the General Store, no matter how mediocre it is. And, honey, remember, it's just a creaky old house. No phantoms, hear?"

"I hear you, Dad." *Don't believe you, though.* I tried for a joke: "I guess you'll be stuck with hospital food tonight.

Maybe you can write an article about salt-free soup. I love
you, Dad. Tell Mom, too." I clicked the END button. The
beeps echoed in the room.

Gabe sprawled out on my bed. "They're okay, just shook
up by the accident."

"What aren't you telling me?" I demanded, scared that
our parents were really hurt worse than they were letting
on, and stuck in a town we couldn't get to, and besides
that, we'd have to stay in this freaky house without them
one more night.

"They're okay," Gabe said again. "We've just got to pull
it together until they get back. Nothing to worry about."

Right, so why did he look so scared?

Sal said, "This is family business. I know when it ain't
my place. I'll just scoot outta here."

"Wait," Gabe said. "We need some answers. But first,
put out that fire, Lila. It's about a hundred degrees in here."

I scurried over to beat the fire dead with a rusty
andiron. Like Daphne and the storm. I turned the air-
conditioning down to sixty.

"Next," Gabe said, "we've gotta get to the bottom of all
this craziness. Sal, you're the key. My sister's seeing stuff
that's, well, not there. I don't want to think she's nuts, so
I'm trying to figure out who's pulling the strings around
here. Tell us straightforward: what's the gimmick?"

"Don't know that word, *gimmick*," she said.

"The show, the ghosts, the ghouly-ghouly stuff for tour-
ists. Who's quarterbacking the whole thing? Camilla?"

"I don't know nothing about football, either," Sal said
stubbornly. She locked her lips until they turned pale pink.

"Talk to us!" Gabe demanded, but Sal just shook her head and rolled her eyes up until only the whites showed. See no evil, speak no evil.

"You talked about a kitchen girl named Eulie," I prompted, trying to loosen Sal's tongue. "And then the girl hacking the storm with an ax this afternoon. You saw it, too, Sal. Tell him."

Gabe laughed. "Hacking a storm. Right. Chopping up the rain and wind like they're firewood? Explain. How can she do it?"

"She *can*." The words burst from Sal's lips. "Wouldn't you, if you could?" She looked at me for approval, and I nodded. "What you know about spirits, Yankee boy, could just about fill a thimble."

"We are *not* Yankees," Gabe protested. "But hey, I'm listening."

Her hands on her skinny hips, Sal said, "Okay, first thing. My grandmama, she says these spirits've got unfinished business in this world. Trying to work it out from the Other Side. Or else they're sticking by watching out for us, or for each other, keeping company."

Gabe closed his eyes, trying to take this news seriously.

"Sometimes they come back 'cause they're plain curious and bored of heaven or wherever they're hanging out, and they wanna stir up a little mischief for kicks." She chuckled. "That's what I'd do if I was a spirit."

"Where are they, exactly?" Gabe asked doubtfully, with his arms crossed over his chest.

"Everywhere!" Sal pointed to the bedpost next to Gabe's head. "There's one of 'em perched right there beside you like a owl. Could be your grandmama who's passed, watching out for you, telling you your folks are going to be okay from that car wreck."

Gabe jerked his head around. "I don't see or hear anything."

"Don't mean she's not there. And over here by my friend Lila? Her angel's a guy. Hasn't been long since he passed. Still fresh." She stared at me, or at something behind me, concentrating real hard, then whispered, "All them broken parts? He got fixed again as soon as he passed over, so don't worry about him."

I whispered to Gabe, "I think she means Roberto."

"Oh, man," he said, shaking his head. Gabe, with his music and baseball, saw the world in predictable patterns— notes on a staff and box score numbers and the distance between the pitcher's mound and the batter's box. The things Sal was talking about, ghosts and spirits, these couldn't be measured or counted. They just *were*, though not for Gabe, not yet, and maybe never.

But I *could* see and hear them.

Chapter Twenty-one
Daphne

First full moon, Birdie took me out to the tree. She made me move out from under it to see the moon clear, no limbs lacing the view. You know how it goes—bad luck if anything streaks across the full moon when you're looking at it. Birdie left me there while she went to go string swamp lilies around the neck of Ketty's baby, who was having a bad time cutting her back teeth. Guess the *spirit* in the swamp lillies did the trick for that little one.

I'd been out there with my tree days and days, learning every inch of him. He was a him all right, by the name of Timberlarken. I didn't go hunting for the name; just heard it whispered one day when I was lying under the shade of his leaves, listening to his rustling leaves, learning his language. Timberlarken. Scared me to shaking the first time I heard his voice calling my name. He said, *Lean your back up against me, Daphne. I'm solid, I can hold you up.* I pressed my back against him, then drew up my legs and leaned my head on his trunk. Heard him say, *But if you take up a knife or a nail, you can easily drive it into my flesh. I can soak up rain and blood.*

Oh, he told me all kinds of things, and he listened, too, while I whispered what I felt deep down inside. All the while Luke Mullin worked in the yard and kept an eye on me, which means he was looking away from me with that lazy eye.

After about a month, I got real good at tree talking.

Timberlarken told me about river currents and the pull of the moon that makes tides over the Gulf. About the rings inside a tree telling you how old the tree is. About how bees collect nectar and turn it into honey inside their own bodies, like *mamans* make milk. About lightning and stardust and sunbursts. He talked like the flowery poems Alice used to read me.

I told Timberlarken about my first *maman*, Henriette, and the daddy I never knew, him being the tree talker I got it from. About how Birdie'd just about given up on me with the healing roots and all, until she delivered me into the skinny limbs of this oak tree. About Molly and Alice and how looking at them made my throat ache with love some days, and other days I'd of been happy to drop them in the well. Told him about how glad I was to be safe under the tree where the Judge wouldn't find me with his swinging lantern.

And I told him about Isaac. "Me and Isaac have got a whole load of tomorrows together," I told Timberlarken. Trees understand about yesterday and tomorrow, since they've got more rings than folks would ever have on their own selves.

Thinking on it now puts me in mind of the time Miss Amelia told me about my name. It was a sunshiny day, so Birdie sent me out back to hang a small wash of kitchen rags. Miss Amelia was out wandering, bundled like a *bébé* head to foot 'cause she didn't want sun beating on her skin, and I wondered how she could breathe, all that gauzy cloth wrapped around her. Birdie had already told me, "Mornings, that poor lady's been filling up the slop jar. She's got a baby growing in her, and she ain't too happy about it, that's a fact."

So, Miss Amelia took to walking and brooding around outside to settle her stomach and her head. I hung a dish towel and peeked at her from behind it. I swear, she was as white as the towel, with her hand on her belly like she was keeping it from spilling out. She came close. I waited for her to nod, so I could speak.

"Morning, ma'am," I said, busying myself with shaking out wrinkles from the wash. Not looking her way, of course.

"I'm feeling poorly," she said with a moan.

"Yes, ma'am. Anything I can do to ease you, Miss Amelia?"

"What ails me isn't going away," she said, sharp and woeful. "Daphne. Did I ever tell you how I came to name you that?"

"No, ma'am." She moved with me down the row of wash, which made me so jittery that I dropped a few clothespins in the grass.

"It's from a story the Greeks tell."

Greeks? I was thinking that must be the plantation out past Livingstons', though nobody ever mentioned the Greek place before.

"A bitter love story," Miss Amelia said.

Well, wasn't every one of them bitter, except me and *mon cher* Isaac? I stuck three clothespins between my lips so I wouldn't say what was on my tongue.

"The god Apollo loved Daphne, but she didn't love him or want his attentions. Apollo wouldn't give up. He kept pursuing her. You can imagine what that's like, can't you, Daphne?"

Was she talking riddles? Like about me and the Judge?

"She begged her father for help."

I guess her father wasn't sold off to another plantation.

By now Miss Amelia was so caught up in her story that she was stooping down to the bucket and handing me up clothespins! Didn't know whether to take them from her or not, her being the missus and me just the washer girl. But I did, I took the clothespins like we were doing the wash together.

"So, her father honored her wishes and turned her into a tree."

"You don't say!" I cried, spitting clothespins, then added, "ma'am."

"Indeed. Her hair became the leaves, her arms the branches, her feet the roots, and her body was covered in bark. That's what I thought of when I first saw you. You were just the color of tender brown bark, so I named you Daphne." She sucked in and let out a big sigh. "You know what kind of tree it was?"

"No, ma'am, I sure couldn't guess," but I liked the thought of me, a tree like Timberlarken.

"It was a laurel," she said. "Not quite a laurel oak, but similar to the very trees this plantation is named for." Suddenly Miss Amelia realized that she'd been handing me clothespins, and she dropped two into the bucket like they were hot potatoes right off the coals. Then she said, almost like she knew I was thinking about Timberlarken, "Live oaks grow to be enormous and very old, but I tell you, Daphne, the laurels don't live long."

With that, she turned away, and in a minute I heard her retching out behind the kitchen garden.

One night, before the Judge came around, I slipped out and took my bedsheet to the tree and slept there under his leaves. Judge wasn't too happy in the morning, but I told him it was just too hot those summer nights sleeping behind the stove. That I could sleep outside where it was breezy, so I'd be fit for making his biscuits and frying his morning beefsteak. I didn't tell him just where I was begging that breeze. He'd of come after me and had Hector

chop down Timberlarken for sure. Anyway, I don't think
the Judge liked me much anymore, and I sure didn't lose
tears over that. Or else he was feeling shame, his wife
being with child and all.

So, my fourth night sleeping under the tree, Timberlarken figured out what I was missing without my even
telling him. He said, *Remove your turban, Daphne.*

I didn't want to. Didn't want Timberlarken to see how
ugly I was under there, but it was a dark, moonless night,
and maybe he wouldn't see the smashed pink open sore
too clear.

I peeled off the hat and leaned slantdickelar to Timberlarken's trunk, the dead side of my head against that tree
so long, so many hours awake and asleep, that some of me
started pressing off onto the smooth bark. Woke up in the
morning and saw a knot in the tree, longer than it was
wide, with swirls around the outside of a small, dark tunnel worming into the tree. The whole knot was oval-shaped,
like the tongue of a spoon, like a seashell.

Like *une oreille.* An ear.

Chapter Twenty-two

Lila

Sal glanced at me, as if to ask, *Can we trust Gabe now?*
"You talking about Daphne, who seems to be hanging
around here, at least that's what some folks swear."

"Tell me you haven't actually seen her," Gabe said quietly.

"I wouldn't say that. I see her now and then, but we
don't have a talk-about-it thing going." She twisted the
hem of my T-shirt, deciding how much more to say. "I feel
stuff from her, though. Stuff, you know?"

"Maybe you should tell me what you know about her,"
Gabe said, "and don't feed me Camilla's line about the
bloody mirror and the ear."

"Yup, I be honest with you, best I can," Sal promised. "She's kind of a restless soul, that one."

"She should be restless," Gabe said. "She killed two girls and their mother. She's not exactly entitled to a free ride in heaven."

Sal stuck her hands on her skinny hips and cinched up her face. "You think she don't hear everybody talking about her poisoning those little white girls, like you just said it, Yankee boy? How you think she feels, hearing that from Miss Camilla every night at nine twenty-two on the dot? Must make her wonder, 'Well, did I do it, or didn't I?'"

"Did she?" I asked.

"Think I know? Hunh-uh. But say she didn't do it."

"Everybody says she did. It's even in the history museum," Gabe reminded us.

"Yup, but history might could be telling itself all backwards and sideways."

I thought a good long while before speaking—not my usual rampage. "You mean, everyone *thinks* Daphne's the murderer, and they've been telling that story to thousands of people, but Daphne's really innocent? Maybe somebody else did it? Maybe Eulie?"

"Don't go blaming Eulie just because she's sweet as horseradish," Sal cautioned us.

Gabe asked, "Okay, then who poisoned those people?"

Sal shrugged. "Might coulda been Daphne, at that."

Gabe tugged at his shirt, which was plastered to his back. "Man, it's hot, and we're getting nowhere."

"It ain't hot," Sal said. "Feel." She put her hand on my

arm. It felt like a slab of meat from the fridge. She started shaking; her teeth chattered.

I didn't feel a bit cold. I reached for the mirror on the dresser. "Look at yourself, Sal. Ice crystals on your eyebrows!"

Waves of cold from her mouth turned the mirror foggy. Gabe slid to the floor between Sal and me and grabbed the mirror. He swiped it across his shirt to clear it and held it up to his own eyes. I looked over his shoulder. That face! And then it was gone as tiny cracks webbed across the mirror until it looked like a mosaic of broken chips.

"Wow! Must have cracked from the cold," Gabe cried, though he still had sweat pooling at his neck.

I wrapped Sal in the quilt just as the cracks healed right before our eyes. A voiceless warning, cold as Alaska, said, "GIT AWAY!"

The mirror shot out of Gabe's hand and shattered on the hardwood floor.

"You heard it, didn't you?" I whispered.

"Clear as a bell," Sal said.

"You, Gabe?"

His eyes blazed and his hands shook. In a choked voice, he murmured, "Yeah, I heard it."

"And saw it?" I asked hopefully, but he shook his head.

The image in the mirror had been as clear as the message. Whatever her name was, she was spitting mad and truly meant for us to stop trying to uncover the secrets of Laurel Oaks.

Well, we wouldn't stop!

Gabe scooped up a thousand crumbs of glass.

I noticed his hands were still shaking. Dueling thoughts flickered across his face. His eyes widened, he opened his arms as if to gather the air around him. I think that's the moment he started to believe in the possibility that spirits really were here at Laurel Oaks. That there were things you couldn't see or measure or explain away.

I'm sure Sal noticed the change in Gabe. She stood in the middle of the room with the quilt twisted tight around her. Her eyes were on the needlepoint sampler.

"Something about it?" I asked.

"Not sure," Sal said.

"Okay, for now just don't go barefoot," I warned, trying to figure out what we *had* seen and heard, even Gabe, and what it had to do with that sampler. "The face in the mirror?" I began.

"My face, or Yankee boy's face?" asked Sal.

"No, the woman."

"What'd she look like?" Sal asked.

"Black, fortyish, round face with, like, pockmarks and a chipped tooth."

"That'd be Eulie," Sal said positively. "It's just how my grandmama sees her."

I suggested, "Maybe we're closing in on a secret that she's guarding with her life."

Gabe looked stunned—he'd finally heard a ghost, but he was still trying to hang on to some of his reasonable doubt. "Guarding with her *life?*" he shouted. "Lila, she's dead!"

Sal said, "You got a nickel?"

"What?" Gabe shook his head in disbelief, but he fished one out of his pocket.

"Call it," she said. "Heads or tails. Call it."

"Heads," I said. "So what?"

"So this." Sal flicked the coin off her thumb and slapped the nickel down on Gabe's arm. "Heads. You win. See? Alive or dead. They're just two sides of a coin. Flip it, and you don't know what's gonna turn up."

Smiling, she dropped the coin into her sock and said, "Wisht I'd asked for a quarter!"

"Can we get back to the mirror thing?" Gabe said. His voice still sounded distant, almost distracted.

"Yup. Well, I ain't saying I know everything, and I don't even know much, but one time I snuck my grandmama into the house while Miss Camilla was over to the store in town. I had a time-and-a-half getting my grandmama up the stairs, her with the osteo-authoritis crippling her. She hobbled up here and passed up every one of the locked doors, heading right to this room. Maude Eberly. Grandmama, she sniffed around it awhile, touched just about everything with those bent fingers hooked like they are. And you know what she said?"

"What? What!" I cried.

That rascal Sal shucked off the quilt, pulled her knees up to her chin, and made a tent of my stretched T-shirt. "You don't want to know, do you? Nah. I guess I'll just head back down to the cellar."

I grabbed her arm. "What did she say about this room?"

"You got a quarter after all, Yankee boy?"

Gabe flipped her another coin, which also disappeared

into her sock. "Woo-wee, I'm gettin' rich today. Well, my grandmama, she said Daphne and Eulie are fighting each other like cat and mouse for this room and anybody stays in it."

Gabe said, "How much is true, and how much do you make up right on the spot?"

She shrugged. "I'd say half. But this half's true. You saying you don't feel it? Them having a tug-of-war?"

Gabe made a circle of the room. "I don't sense a battle, do you, Lila?"

"Maybe you don't have no sense," Sal said with a chuckle. "Grandmama says they both of 'em got a thing they have to prove out, and they know there's something in this room that'll do it."

Her eyes scanned the whole space—the love seat, the vanity, the chandelier, the hat rack—and they came back around to the sampler on the wall. "Just a wild guess, but I'd say that ugly old thing figures in it somehow."

I took the needlepoint down again. Nothing behind it, and no opening to a secret cubbyhole. I set it back on the hook, and it slipped sideways again.

"Could be wrong," Sal said, grinning. "Anyways, I better get my soggy clothes from the bathroom and go on downstairs before Miss Camilla sends the Loosiana Child Welfare after me." She started for the door. "Lila-girl, tell your stubborn brother what my grandmama said about talking to trees, because I'm thinking if you really want to know what happened with the poisoning of those little white girls and all, ask that big old oak tree out front. Daphne's tree."

Chapter Twenty-three

Daphne

Now Lila knows Timberlarken's my tree, just like Birdie did even before I knew, myself. That Birdie, I tell you, wasn't anybody who didn't love her back then. Long about 1840, Birdie was at the top of her conjure woman powers. She could do just about anything a body needed. She got ahold of the Judge's whiskey cabinet key and poured a little from each bottle into a jam jar that she kept out in the corn crib. So when Therese started showing pouchy about her middle one winter, Birdie had her to put a spoonful of whiskey in her left shoe every day, and grind that into her heel until it went dry, to keep evil spirits from hurting

Therese's bébé-to-come. Few months later, Therese had a sturdy little piglet of a boy squalling on her shoulder, which was a big time at our place for white and black folks alike. For us, it meant we'd done something fine, brought new life into the light of day, shored up our numbers because Oncle Joe wasn't long for the world, and Tante Drucilla was already panting like a dog when she walked from her shack to the house.

For the Judge and Miss Amelia up at the big house, it meant one more slave they owned who'd grow up to be worth something, only not the way *we* counted worth.

Got to thinking about a body's worth one day when a thought struck me hard about Birdie. In my eyes, she'd always been good and strong, but I had to admit, as I got bigger, that Birdie wasn't just a healing conjure woman, no. Truth to tell, she was two-handed. Means she could do right-hand work to heal somebody or take away a hex some other hoodoo conjurer had fixed, but she could also do left-hand work. She could set a mojo on a person and make terrible things happen to him.

I saw it with my own eyes. It was that breathing time between dinner and supper, when Birdie had a spare minute or five to herself. Sometimes she went down to the quarters to sprawl herself out on Tante Drucilla's cot, especially when her feet were swollen up big as Sunday hams and hanging over her shoes. But this one day, I was down peeking in the smokehouse window with Molly standing on my shoulders, both of us catching a glorious whiff of smoking meat, when I spied Birdie out back there, stooped over a tree stump.

I whispered to Molly, "Let's sneak up on Birdie, want to?" and she was happy to, so we tiptoed over quiet as field mice. Now, Birdie was stone-deaf in one ear, so she didn't hear us coming, and she didn't see us, neither, because she was thinking so hard about whatever it was she was do-ing. If it wasn't for how much time I'd spent around Birdie, I might've taken her for someone else that day. Her cheeks were pulled up into plaits, her eyes were narrow slits, and she had both her lips tucked under and locked tight, as she moaned out some tune I'd never heard before. All the while, she worked her sure hands over some tin cups, but her hands were covered with rags.

I think the look of her put a scare in Molly, because she tucked her face into my dress, and I didn't blame her a bit.

Next thing I noticed were some pretty buttery-yellow flowers on the tree stump, and some others dried up brownish-gold, and Birdie was mashing and smashing them into something powdery.

"What are you doing, Birdie?" I asked, and she jumped like a jackrabbit, or as high as a woman her heft could.

She stared at me through those slits and finally said, "Fetch the child to the house and come on back." Her voice didn't sound Birdie-like at all, like it was coming from deeper in her chest than her usual.

Well, I carried Molly back to the house and gave her a book to look at and didn't know if it was upside down or right side up. Then I raced back to Birdie fast as my bare feet could carry me over the dirt that was knotty with tree roots.

"Might as well learn it," Birdie said, pinching a dried flower into crumbs. "Better know what's 'lander, and what ain't." She held up one of the pretty yellow flowers, fresh-picked. Oleander, the only flower I knew for sure. "Poison through and through," Birdie said.

"I know it, Birdie, but what are you doing with it?"

"Fixing a hex," she said.

"You mean *un*fixing a hex, don't you?"

"No, child. Sure 'nuf, 'lander's good for healing skin raw from the whip." She picked up a handful of dried leaves and crumbled them into one of her cups. "Then some days, you jest got to have a killing poison you can count on to do the trick quick and sure."

Shocked me to hear it, but I kept my mouth shut for once.

"Conjuring ain't all for good, child. I can set a mojo on a person and make him feel like reptiles was crawling in-side his skin; make a woman break a leg; make her insides burn up raw."

"Birdie!" I cried.

This time she snapped open a green stalk oozing milky sap. "Pure poison," she said, squeezing the sap into another cup. "All it takes is a drop or two, right place, right time."

I watched, shaking all over. Then all of a sudden, it felt like her whole self changed. Eyes opened up wide again, lips went back pink and full and ready to laugh. She scooped up the flowers, stalks, dried-up crumbs, the cups, her rags, and laid them on a hammock she made of her curled-over apron. "Always got to be ready," is all she said, and we walked back to the house, shoulders apart.

After that day, I looked at Birdie different, but I loved her just the same.

Chapter Twenty-four

Lila

Daphne's tree loomed above all the others in front of the house. As eager as I'd been to climb it earlier in the day, now I stood before it like a statue, feeling dumb. A talking tree, *really!* But then I remembered the mysterious voice I'd heard earlier. This ancient tree had witnessed everything at Laurel Oaks Plantation and could tell all—if, like Sal said, a person knew how to listen.

Gabe stood at the bottom of the tree, gazing straight up. "Real tall tree," he said anxiously. He's a little scared of heights, though he'd never admit that.

I remembered one of Dad's favorite corny sayings, *You*

can't see the forest for the trees. It had never made sense to me before, but now it did. I backed away, ten, twenty feet, and walked all around the tree slowly. And that reminded me of the strange, bald circle around the shack out in the field.

"You game to climb it?" I asked Gabe, who was on the other side of the trunk. Instead of answering, he eased himself into the climb by describing what he saw, as if words could tame the tree. "Lot of snaky-looking branches. Some jagged limbs that might have been snapped off by lightning, or that storm this afternoon."

I was eager to monkey-climb my way into those thick branches, but I looked up, trying to see the tree through new eyes, my brother's eyes.

Then I spotted something that took my breath away. Was it what it *appeared* to be? I stared up until my vision blurred, but yes! Way high up, not cut into the tree, but on top of the bark, there was a long, gently curved, brownish-pink scar. Unmistakably Daphne's mark. "Gabe, over here! Look up."

He ran around to my side of the tree.

"Higher!" I yelled. "Keep looking, you'll see it."

Gabe squinted, framed his vision in a neat square formed by his hands. "Leaves. Moss. Squirrel holes."

"Right there!" I pointed way high up in the tree, and his eyes followed the slant of my arm.

"Yeah, a few knots, a lot of leaves— Oh, man!"

"You see it?"

"Oh, man, it looks like a giant ear just stuck right onto the tree."

"It's Daphne's ear," I said quietly. "How did it get there? I'm going up. Give me a boost."

Gabe dropped to his knees to make a step of his laced hands. Shaking with excitement, I planted my foot squarely and hoisted myself up to grasp the lowest branch I could chin up on. From there it was easy, using knots as footholds. I reached a branch broad and solid enough to support myself over the long haul, in case I had to spend the whole night here waiting. *Waiting for what?*

The branch was below the ear scar, but I could reach way up and barely run my finger over the rough bottom of Daphne's ear, rubbing it like the belly of Aladdin's lamp, expecting something magical to appear.

Expecting the tree to speak. It held its tongue.

"What's it like up close?" Gabe called from the base of the oak.

"Come up and see for yourself."

I heard him scamper up the first few feet, then settle onto a branch close enough to the ground for a quick getaway. "I can see from here," he said. "Send bulletins."

"Shh, I'm listening." But all I heard was the rustling of leaves in the wind, a faint crackling of dry bark, and the sound of a brittle twig giving way, no louder than a snapping tortilla chip.

And then I gasped.

"What?" Gabe called up to me.

A tsunami of grief washed over me. "You getting it, Gabe?"

"What?"

"Something awful, something horribly violent happened

in this tree. It sounds nutso, I know, but the tree is real sad about it."

"Come down, Lila," Gabe demanded, jumping to the ground. "I don't trust a tree that has feelings any more than I'd trust a person who sprouted leaves."

Reluctantly, I began sliding down the trunk, until my shoe caught in a giant knot, with my other leg stretched to a limb way lower. "I'm stuck. My shoe!"

"Just yank your foot out of the shoe," Gabe advised. "Get out of that tree!"

"No way am I leaving a brand-new Nike up here." I tried to loosen its grip on my foot, but I couldn't get the shoe out, and my ankle twisted at a sick angle. I tried pulling my other leg up to the same height, trusting all my weight to three toes and the promise of stiff new sneakers. My stretched leg was beginning to wobble from the strain, along with a sharp pang in my hip. What if the branch supporting my toes gave way? Branches snap; leg bones snap, too, like twigs! A muscle spasm in my calf told me I was in trouble. Me, the first one on the rope walk at Camp Lakawana every year. Me, who'd fought total strangers to get the front position white-water rafting. "Gabe!" I shrieked.

Stay very calm. Let go. I will support you. Relax your muscles.

"Easy for you to say. You're not being split in two!"

"I didn't say anything," Gabe yelled.

The voice of the tree?

"I'm coming up there," Gabe said.

"You? You don't even climb the back fence at home."

I shut up. Didn't want to discourage him. Huffing and grunting and muttering himself into bravery, my brother slowly scaled the tree—and stomped on my hand.

"Ouch!" But the pain was nothing compared to the relief of his nearness.

He tore at the knothole with his bare hands to widen it and wrestled my shoe loose. I needed a minute to get my muscles working again, then shimmied down the knotty tree trunk.

Gabe jumped down beside me, swearing, "I am *never* doing anything that stupid again."

I gave him a big hug, which embarrassed him. I thought about the Bible, how people got new names when monumental things happened to change them. This had to be one of those time. "From now on this is the Ear Tree."

"Yeah," Gabe said grudgingly, "but I didn't hear it talk. I guess its bark is worse than its bite."

"You don't know how to listen," I said smugly, but in my heart I wondered if I really knew how and if the tree would share its secrets with me.

Gabe said, "Okay, reality check. It's almost dark, so we're going up to your room. We're going to play checkers like normal people."

"I call red."

"Whatever. And then we'll wait to see what turns up. Maybe a ghoul will walk through the walls, or something transparent will slither out of the air-conditioning vent."

I knew by his tone that the jokes were meant to reassure us both—meaning even my big brother was scared stiff now.

Upstairs, Gabe ducked down the hall to the bathroom. The flushing of the toilet sounded like a train rumbling through a tunnel. I watched the light in the hall sputter, remembering the warning in the note that had greeted us— only yesterday?—the minute the last light in the house is snuffed out, the spirits are released.

Well, apparently the spirits forgot to read the note, because they sure seemed to be on the loose already.

We set up the game on the floor. It was the longest time either of us had survived without a TV. Which left too much time to think about things like Mom and Dad. Dad had broken ribs, and what else wasn't he telling us? Mom's concussion—I wasn't sure what that was, but it sounded serious.

"Hey, Gabe, what's a concussion?"

He began one of his big-brother lectures: "It's a violent blow to the soft tissue—"

"Just tell me if she's going to have brain damage."

He rolled his eyes. "You always expect the worst." I could see he was still shaken by the tree stuff, and *he* hadn't even heard the voice.

Keep busy, that was our plan. We poured the checkers out on the floor. "Watch for glass crumbs," I warned as we lined up our pieces on the dark squares. I made the first move. Gabe had an infuriating way of *thinking* about each move like in chess, which I never had the patience for. I waited for him to plot out his whole attack across the board before his first move.

"Hey, Gabe, that needlepoint thing on the wall. It's spooky, don't you think? Sal thinks so."

He stared at the board. "Spooky, compared to a tree that talks? Spooky, compared to a mirror shouting 'GIT AWAY'? Spooky compared to dead people showing up and vanishing before your eyes? This whole place is a freak show." He made his first move and looked up.

I slid my checker in a flash. It's just a silly game; why would anybody care who wins?

Besides, I had more interesting things on my mind. "Spooky, like there's got to be something behind it." I told him about the cat's bizarre reaction to the sampler when I took it off the wall. "Maybe that's what Daphne was trying to point me toward when she begged me to *find the babies . . . the babies in the wall.* Don't forget, Camilla said something was hidden in this room a long time ago."

I got up and yanked the frame off the hook. Inspecting more closely than I had before, I spotted a circle of tiny holes in the wall. I ran my finger over the holes; bits of wallpaper flaked off. Curious.

"Just turn that thing to the wall with the stupid words facing in," Gabe said.

There was a knock on the door. Gabe and I both jumped. Our nerves were shot.

But it was only Sal, with a stack of baloney sandwiches and two cans of Pepsi. "I told Miss Camilla about your folks staying over in Baton Rouge on accounta the wreck. She sent this up for you."

I dragged Sal and her tray into the room. Dad didn't believe in baloney and white bread in our house any more than he approved of store-bought muffins, so these sandwiches were a major treat. Gabe had already left his teeth marks in a big half-moon bite.

So much for being a vegetarian. With a mouth full of greasy baloney and pulpy Wonder Bread, I said, "Guess what, Sal. We saw it, the thing on the tree."

"What thing?" she asked.

I whispered conspiratorially, "What do you think? Daphne's ear!"

"Her ear? On that tree? This a Yankee joke I ain't getting? Hey, Miss Camilla says to tell you it's almost nine o'clock. Some weekend folks from Delaware are coming over. Not staying here, just taking the Candlelight Tour."

"We'll be right down," I said, popping the top on a Pepsi can.

"Yup, that's just it. Miss Camilla sent up this supper to tell you don't come down and spoil it for the Delaware folks." Sal snickered mischievously. "She don't like you!"

After our wonderful gourmet supper, we played three more games of checkers, and our all-time favorite family game where you ask stuff like, would you rather eat a plate full of camel tongues or drink a bucket of monkey spit? And which is worse, being dunked in boiling water or boiling oil?

Then, totally grossed out, we decided Gabe should sleep on that miserably uncomfortable love seat in my room, since we'd be alone in the house, if you didn't count Camilla and Sal in the basement. I had the first turn in the bathroom while Gabe went across the hall to get his pillow and comforter and his trombone case.

He said, "We'll barricade ourselves in here until sunrise."

"But do *not* play reveille on that thing tomorrow morning. This isn't Camp Lakawana."

We were both trying so hard to pretend everything was normal, when nothing was, as we locked the door and windows and scooched the love seat across the room until it totally blocked the door.

Chapter Twenty-five

Daphne

Next thing I know, Birdie's put a hex on Sansant, Roweena's man, who was pickled in home-brewed huckleberry wine and hanging around with Eulie's son, Tom. Guess Sansant was just plain scared about being a daddy. Lot of our men were, 'cause what could they do to take care of their *bébés*? Nothing, you know how it is. So, Sansant, he'd been stumbling home drunk when Roweena's babyload was hanging practically to her knees.

We watched Sansant from out behind their shack, Birdie and me. In a minute that man was crawling on all fours like a hound, barking and howling at the moon and crying out, "I been whammied! I been whammied! Can't see nothing!"

"That drunk can see, all right," Birdie whispered to me, "but he seeing like a bird, out the sides of his eyes, not straight on."

Well, his yelping brought people running, left and right—Oncle Joe, Isaac, Therese and Shem, Anjou, Tante Drucilla—all of them, coming to see what the commotion was all about. I even saw Luke Mullin watching from the shadows, 'cause nobody wanted to see his free man cross-eyed face too close.

Eulie tore out of her shack, shrieking like a banshee. "Birdie, what you done to my boy? Oh, it's just Sansant."

And poor Sansant, he was baying like a lonesome hound one minute, the next minute shouting, "I been whammied; somebody help me."

Isaac found us behind the shack. I watched his pretty eyes pierce the darkness while he whispered, "Mama? You done this to Sansant?"

I nodded. Birdie kept it to herself.

"We got to find the charm," Oncle Joe said, over in the circle around Sansant. "Must be here nearby somewheres. Got to dig it up and burn it."

Isaac joined the rest of them. "Take care. Whoever it was called for this whammy, what you do to it, you gonna do to him. Maybe her."

Oh, I sure knew what he meant. Burn the gris-gris bag, and Roweena burns up in a fire in a day or two. Throw the bag in the river, and Roweena drowns, along with her *bébé.* "Do something, Birdie!" I said under my breath. "Make it stop!"

But Birdie just folded her powerful arms across her chest and refused to do a thing. My Birdie. *Mon cher* Isaac's Birdie. Shocked me to the core, this evil magic did, and Birdie beside me as immovable as a giant boulder.

Somebody had to look after Roweena and that innocent baby. Birdie grabbed my arm in her iron fist, but I broke away and stepped out from behind the house. I sank to my knees and began scrabbling at the ground with my bare fingers until they were raw and bloody, but I got that mojo bag, ripped it open, stood up, spread out my arms, twirled three times, and let all that foolish stuff scatter to the wind—the dirt from Sansant's footprint, the bones and a hairball of a black cat, a dried-up lizard's skin, the rattle of a snake, and some of Birdie's confounded herbs. You could smell the cayenne floating in the air. Most all these things Birdie kept locked in a chest in her room, just the way Doc Ramsey stowed liniment and cod liver oil and paregoric in his leathery bag he took calling on folks.

Isaac flashed me a secret smile as he dusted Sansant off. "You ain't no dog," he said, and stood Sansant upright like a man. Eulie brought out a tin cup of thick chicory coffee and poured it down Sansant's throat. Isaac and Tom walked Sansant back and forth until the coffee and the night breeze sobered him up.

Roweena thought it was safe to come out then. Said in her tweety little voice, "So, you get the idea, Sansant?"

He looked at her with new eyes, gonna-be-a-father eyes.

She said, "You stay clearheaded and not be rotting your gut with that wild boy brew no more, hear?"

"I swear it, Miss Roweena," we all heard him say.

Tante Drucilla placed a Bible under his hand. The pages were all curled up, and she couldn't read a word of it, but she knew from Sunday church that you couldn't lie with your hand on that fine paper. "Say it again, Sansant, loud enough for Jesus to hear up in heaven," she commanded, and he did.

Everybody was *gumbo-ya-ya*, yammering all at once. Then Roweena took Sansant home, and Eulie shooed Tom back into their shack, and you know how it goes, they all scattered to their own place. I turned to find Birdie. She'd gone.

Now that all the excitement was over, I went chilled to the bone, even in the warm, sticky night, thinking about how easily Birdie could turn good to evil. Sure, she did it to look after Roweena and the *bébé*, but what else could her kind of fierce power do?

I was curled under my tree that night when Birdie came around. Saw her just as a dark patch at first, but I knew by the shape that it was Birdie and not anybody else looking for me. She stood over me, scaring me down to the blood pumping in my veins.

I pressed my eyes shut like a possum, but there was no fooling Birdie. She said, "What you done, child, was pure foolishness. You don't know what you're messing with out there. Could of done harm like you never seen, scattering my mojo bag that way."

I wanted to say, *I'm sorry, Birdie, truly I am.* But I wasn't.

"You got anything to say to me, child?" There wasn't an ounce of gentle in her voice, scaring me even more, but not a word passed my lips.

Finally Birdie muttered, "You sure ain't no conjure woman your own self."

She slapped my tree a good one. I watched her turn until her wide back was to me, and I barely heard these words, which maybe she didn't even want me to hear:

"But you got your own kind of magic that folks has got to reckon with, talking to this tree of yours. Shouldn't never have took you here, that's a fact."

True? She shouldn't have put me and that tree together? I didn't have the *voudoun* like Birdie or Eulie, but Timberlarken and me? Birdie was right, we had our own kind of magic.

What happened in that tree a time later, it was powerful bad and it was powerful good. Sal suspicions, but she doesn't know the whole story. Lila's the one who's gonna get an earful. If Timberlarken's up to talking, and Lila's up to listening, no telling what'll come out. I'm moving closer, even if it scares me to, 'cause I have to know what she hears.

It pains me to think that I've passed on to the next world without delivering Miss Amelia's *bébés* to the right person, like I promised her. But then, who is the right person, being as Miss Amelia's girls are up in heaven? If Lila-with-the-spiny-hair is the right one, I got to find out for sure. Meaning, if Timberlarken tells her all his secrets, and she doesn't run away screaming like somebody Birdie'd put a hex on.

Chapter Twenty-six

Lila

Saturday morning the rooster woke me again, and my first thought was, did Daphne come to me last night? I searched my brain but couldn't pull up even a wisp of memory from the night's dreams, as though I'd totally disappeared into the dark. My face felt stretched and elastic, with two raw places biting at the corners of my mouth, like after a marathon orthodontist appointment.

Sunshine gradually seeped into the room. I parted the mosquito net and flung my leg over to slide out of bed. I ached all over. Coming down with the flu? My body felt sore and stiff, as if an Arabian steed had been riding *me* all night, and the raw places at the corners of my mouth were where the horse had locked its bit into me. Now, where would I come up with a freaky idea like that? I did a few stretches to loosen myself up and let the morning breeze at the window oil my achy body.

Gabe had apparently fallen off the short couch overnight and was stretched out in his jeans, on the floor, on top of his quilt.

The rooster crowed again, closer this time. But it wasn't coming from outside! It seemed to be coming from behind the big blank space of brighter wallpaper where the sampler had hung. I remembered taking the thing down the night before and turning its face to the wall. Where was it? Gabe must have moved it, but why? Suddenly it was absolutely essential that I find that sampler.

"Gabe! Wake up. Where's the wall hanging?"

"Lemme sleep," Gabe begged, pulling his pillow over his head.

I yanked on his big toe, which he hates. "Up, Gabe. I need to know where the sampler is, pronto!"

With his head still buried, he pulled his toe back and stuck his arm out toward the wall.

"No, it's not there, or anywhere. Did you put it out in the hall?"

Gabe flopped over on his back. "Why would I do that?"

"Well, it can't just vanish."

"Things *do* around here," he grumbled.

"I'm sure I left it propped up slantdickelar against the wall."

"What did you just say? Slantdickelar?"

"Hunh? I didn't say that."

Gabe yawned wide. Morning breath. "Okay, whatever, I'm up, but until I brush my teeth, I'm not awake." He moved the love seat to open the door and padded down the hall to the bathroom.

Frantically, I looked under the bed, in the wardrobe, behind the couch, with my achy body protesting every bend. No sign of the sampler, and why was it so important that I find it, anyway? I didn't even like the thing.

My cell phone rang. So early? I ran for it, saw that it was a 225 area code, Summit Hospital. "Dad? Anything wrong?"

"No, honey, we're okay. As soon as the doctor comes by, she'll release us."

"You scared me. It's so early."

"I know. Hospitals have no regard for normal sleeping cycles. I just wanted to reassure you that Mom and I are mending, despite the dreadful green Jell-O and gray beans on our trays last night. How about there, you and Gabe? What did you do about dinner?"

"Room service," I said, skipping the baloney part. "Then we played the bucket-of-monkey-spit game half the night."

"Always fun," Dad said, and it was good to hear the playfulness in his voice. "Mom's in the bed across the room. Say something, Emily." I heard a faint *hi*, then Dad again. "We should be back around noon, with a decent lunch for us all. 'Gator tail's a delicacy around here, with a side of red beans and dirty rice. How does that sound?"

Yes, he was was fine, even with cracked ribs! "Thanks, but I'll have a good old burger and fries, okay? Bye, Dad."

I flipped the phone shut and curled into the love

seat, massaging my sore muscles. I spotted a corner of
something on top of the canopy over the bed. I climbed
up on the footboard and slid the frame closer so I could
pull it down. Gabe swore he hadn't moved it. Did I?
Sure, like I wouldn't remember doing such a thing? But
then I thought about feeling that I'd *disappeared* all
night. Could I have done something like that and not know
it? Great, I could add sleepwalking to my new list of insane
behaviors.

Maybe I *was* losing it. I stomped around the room to
make sure it was all solid beneath my feet.

The rooster again. "Give it up," I yelled—and put my
ear to the blank spot on the wall. Yes!

When Gabe came back, I made him listen at the wall.
"And don't tell me you don't hear anything."

His eyes popped open in surprise. "Sounds like a
rooster."

"Yippee! I'm not nuts!"

"You thinking they keep live animals in the next
room? Nah, that's impossible."

"Let's go!"

We dashed into the hall and banged on the door of the
next room. No animals squawked their protests. Gabe
took his Albuquerque Public Library card out of his wal-
let and jiggled it around in the space between the door
and the doorjamb until he worked the lock open.

The crowing was clearer than ever. We tore through
the room, searching the closet, under the bed, behind the
dresser, even in the drawers, and there were no live animals,
or even dead ones in the room.

"Darn," I murmured. "I was so sure."

"Back to Maude Eberly," Gabe said, sounding even more disappointed than I was.

We sat on his quilt, trying to make some sense of the rooster call, which was now louder and more demanding than ever, as if the bird wouldn't shut up until we found him and muzzled him.

Gabe got up and put his ear to the wall again. "These six pinholes, what do you think they're all about?"

I stood next to him, tracing the six tiny holes in a perfect circle around the picture hook. Like the clearing around the shack, like the circle around the oak that led me to find Daphne's ear. I thought about Mom saying that the circle is a universal symbol, and Roberto once telling me, *My people believe that all of nature is spirit, a circle with no beginning and no end.*

And then I felt something drawing me across the room to the hat rack, to the long pin of the peacock-feather hat.

"What? What're you doing with that pin?" Gabe asked.

I couldn't speak. As though in a trance, I walked slowly back to the clear place where the sampler had hung and stuck the stiletto point into the first of the six holes, the second one, the third, fourth, fifth. "Last chance," I said, holding my breath as I slid the pin into the sixth hole.

A satisfying snick told us that *something* had happened. The wall slid open at the wallpaper seam, revealing a narrow alcove thick with dust.

Chapter Twenty-seven

Daphne

Back when I breathed air, Saturday night used to be the best time around here. The field hands knew they'd have off 'til sunrise Monday, a whole day and two nights to ease their aching backs and blistery fingers. After supper, Birdie and I'd go down to the quarters. There'd be soup-kettle drummers and whistlers and Oncle Joe had an old fiddle with about two strings left on it. All of us would be dancing, even the babies, even the old *tantes*. Hector, the overseer, he'd go off for some spooning with his wife at Livingstons' place every Saturday night, so we

knew the bull whip wouldn't be cracking, no matter how
much we whooped it up at our ball.

On a good night, we'd sop up corn bread in the juices
of possum stew. The Judge didn't like us hunting possum.
He was funny that way. But that didn't stop Anjou and
Sansant and them from loading up their traps of a night.
Hour, two later, they'd bring a whole gunny sack home,
dripping blood. Therese and Roweena and the other women,
they'd be up half the night skinning and cooking those
things. They'd have to close all the windows and doors so
nobody up at the house would catch a whiff. Ooh, how I
miss a good possum stew!

Nowadays, folks show up here every Saturday night
hunting, all right, but not for possum, and not with guns
or traps. Call themselves ghost-hunters. They're set on
snaring us with their cameras and their voice-catching
contraptions. Every one of them itches to see me clinging
to the side of the house like a barnacle to a fishing boat. I
heard somebody caught a picture like that, and it's over at
the museum in town.

Lots of 'em come hoping to see Alice and Molly swinging their white shiny shoes from off the roof, or they're
hoping to hear Mr. Gladstone stumbling up to the twelfth
step to gasp his last.

Birdie's whole self would be doubled over laughing if
she knew that these Saturday night folks pay money to
catch sight of us! Other folks have scales over their eyes,
but Lila, she sees clear, that one.

Wish she could of known Birdie. Birdie could do anything she set her mind to. She could pull splinters out of a

child's foot by wrapping it in raw pork. She could ease the rheumatism of all those back-bent cotton pickers with a raw potato, a rub of rattlesnake oil or alligator fat, a snake-skin wrap, an oleander salve.

She could do anything, left hand or right, except keep her own self from dying. All the signs were there that day, during those winter months between my ear being gone and the little girls going home to Jerusalem. I knew it was coming, because of the mirror.

One day when Miss Amelia and the girls had gone visiting the Livingstons over to Aubergine House, I went up to Miss Amelia's room to dust her army of perfume bottles, tuck her bed tight the way she liked it, tight enough to bounce a stone off it. Down on all fours, I felt around for her house shoes kicked under the bed, to set them right where her feet would first touch the floor next morn-ing. I stretched my arm way, way under the bed until I felt it—the box I knew was hiding under there. Listened to be sure nobody was coming, and I pulled that box out to smell its fine cowhide, to run my fingers over the cool gold band around it that ended in a tiny keyhole. But not *just* to smell and feel of it, because I'd already gotten the key out of her Emporium hatbox up on the closet shelf. Turned the key, and there they were, her *bébés*. I hefted them, sur-prised all over again how heavy they were, about like a great piece of granite rock, even though I could hold them right in the palm of my hand. Miss Amelia's beautiful golden *bébés*. And me swearing to look after them if Miss Amelia couldn't.

Now, why'd I go and promise that? I s'pose because I

felt sorry for Miss Amelia, fancying herself a Yankee lady here in the swamplands. Didn't help that she had a husband with a wandering eye, and I'm not talking about the kind of wandering eye Luke Mullin had. Since I was the one who caught the Judge's eye, I felt like I owed Miss Amelia something even years later. What else did I have to give her but my promise? And Birdie always said a woman's word should be worth something more than soot that flies up the chimney.

Footsteps. I laid those *bébés* back in the velvety lining of the box and shoved the box under the bed. Jumped up and ran to Miss Amelia's chest o' drawers just as Birdie opened the door.

"Checking to see if you is up to no good," she said, smiling at me as I waved the feather duster over those crystal bottles like I was beating off a bad smell. I looked in the mirror. My turban was all askew from gophering under the bed after that box. Birdie came up behind me and gently pulled it over the ugly place, pink and raw, where an ear used to grow. And then it happened: we both looked in the mirror at the same time. Heard it crack, but you couldn't see a line on the looking glass. Very bad sign. I felt Birdie's hands trembling on my head.

We both knew that, come morning, she was going to be dead, or I was, one.

Chapter Twenty-eight

Lila

"What have we here?" Gabe said with glee as the dusty alcove in the wall was revealed.

Inside stood a small leather box less than a foot wide and maybe eight inches high at the peak of its rounded dome, which was bisected by a lath of golden brass.

"It looks like an elf-sized treasure chest, Gabe."

"Or a mouse's coffin."

Gabe started to reach into the alcove until I yelled, "Wait! Maybe it's booby-trapped inside there."

He yanked his arm back.

I blew dust off the small dome, to reveal a golden clasp

with a tiny keyhole. The treasure chest was lots heavier than I'd expected. "Feels like it's full of gold bars."

"We're rich beyond our wildest dreams," Gabe said. "And what if it does have gold ingots and pirates' doubloons and stuff like that in it? Tell me we don't have to turn it in."

My heart thudded with anticipation. Whatever was inside that heavy chest was important, a secret that had been hidden there for a long time. Daphne's secret? It could have been anybody's, Eulie's maybe, or Luke's, or even Amelia Nethercott's. How would I ever know?—unless we opened the chest.

"You see anything else in this little wall pocket, Lila? Any signs of things like the babies Daphne was talking about?" Gabe gingerly stuck a finger into the alcove, then his whole hand. Nothing exploded or sounded an alarm, so he reached over for my sheet and used it to sweep centuries of dust out of the alcove.

"You could have used your own—" I stopped as I saw him sweep out a shriveled clump of something black and reddish, and it would have burst into crumbs if he hadn't caught it an inch from the hardwood floor. "Eeuw, what is it?"

Gabe held it in the flat of his hand. I examined the clump—and recognized a yellowish beak and something dark red that resembled dried wattles.

"Omigod, you know what that is?" I cried. "It's the head of a rooster!"

"Can't be the one we heard crowing," Gabe said, obviously blown away by the ugly object now depositing a mess of decomposed feathers in his palm. "This thing's been dead for about a hundred years. It's mummified."

"Try a hundred and seventy years," I murmured, offering Gabe a milkglass ashtray as a final resting place for the shriveled rooster head. He gently slid it off his palm. Powdery dust flew.

"Now we've *got* to open the treasure chest, but how, Gabe? Bite the clasp off?"

He flashed a metal smile. "I don't think the ortho would appreciate me chewing the thing open. Use *your* teeth, Lila."

"Here's a brilliant idea. Why don't we try a key, instead?"

"Ingenious," Gabe confirmed. "Problem is, we don't have one that fits."

"There must be a key hidden in there somewhere." I felt all around the inside wall and low ceiling of the alcove for a bump, a hidden niche, something taped or glued or plastered to the surface, but only smooth walls revealed themselves, covered in the same rosy paper as the rest of the room, only brighter, since they'd never seen sunlight.

Gabe said, "Maybe the hat pin's the key to the box, too."

"Not a chance. This keyhole's way bigger than the pinholes in the wall." I sank back against the bed frame with the Fragrant Rose sampler on my lap. Turned it over. The paper backing over the wood frame had gone brittle with age and was flaking at the corners. "Wait a minute. The hat pin *might* be the key. Gimme it."

Gabe handed me the pin, which I used to slice the paper along the hard edge of the wood, then peeled the paper back like skinning an animal. Under it lay the rough-wood skeleton of the frame.

And a tiny old-fashioned key glued to the backside of the sampler.

Gabe snatched the hat pin out of my hand and began picking at the glue to free the key.

"Shh, did you hear that?" I asked.

"What?"

"Sounded like a deep sigh."

"Wind," Gabe said.

"Inside? I don't think so."

Gabe tried to get the key into the treasure chest. "My fingers are too big, and I can't even jam it in," he muttered with his teeth clenched.

I shoved him aside and turned the key upside down. It slid right into place, like a knife through warm butter.

"Bingo!" shouted Gabe.

Chapter Twenty-nine
Daphne

They found Miss Amelia's leathery box with the *bébés* inside! Gives me the shakes wondering what they're going to do with them. Wish I had Birdie here with me now, telling me, "Be patient, child, everything gonna be turning out like it s'pose to."

Sunup the morning after we both looked in the mirror at the same time, Birdie passed. Miss Amelia was sorely grieved. You'd think she'd lost her own *maman*. Her tears kept coming and coming while she helped Eulie and me cover all the mirrors in the house, stop all the clocks, and

light up more candles than you ever did see. Eulie seemed
to be about the only one who could dry Miss Amelia's tears,
always handing her a fresh lilac handkerchief pressed with
rose water.

"Oh, Daphne," hollered Molly, "whatever will we do
without Birdie? She's been here all my whole life long."
The child clung to me like a ball of cotton, and Alice on
my other side, her little peach-colored face pulled tight
across her high Cambridge cheekbones that Miss Amelia
was always pointing to with pride. Those two girls stared
at Birdie laid out on the kitchen floor with Miss Amelia's
lap robe pulled up to her chin, and just wailed like cats in
the rain.

Eulie barked, "Git away, let her rest in peace!" She
went after Miss Amelia, staring at her outside the parlor
until Miss Amelia said, "Yes?" Dabbing at her red eyes.

So Eulie said, "Pardon the commotion, Miss Amelia,
but your girls gonna get the evil spirits if'n they keep
looking at poor Birdie laying there dead on the floor."

I scrambled to pull the girls away from Birdie so Isaac
could take his *maman* down to Sabina's house for the washing. Sabina was the one who saw our folks into the next
world, and everything I did for Birdie, she watched me
like a hawk. You know how it goes—you can't be too careful about dead folks.

But first I washed Birdie limb by limb my own self and
placed the wash water under the bed, like you're s'pose
to do, like nobody did for me, unless you count having a
watery river grave *washing.*

Père Jacques came calling, asking about the Vigil and

blessing Miss Amelia while she cried and cried. Since Birdie was one of us, and not one of *them*, there wouldn't be a big church funeral of course, but we wouldn't of wanted one anyway. Birdie'd gone home. That was enough for us.

Eulie squeezed out fake tears like one of those Bible crocodiles from Noah's Ark. Ketty cried, and Tante Drucilla, and Roweena and Anjou. *Mon cher* Isaac, the last of Birdie's children at our place, kept wiping away tears with the corner of his shirt. "Gone home. Gone to a better place," they all murmured, but cried just the same.

But I was dry-eyed. My tears had all dried up and crumbled; felt like grains of salt scratching at the inside of my eyes and heart.

Down to Sabina's, I loosened and combed out Birdie's hair. If you leave the hair plaited, *Papa le Bas,* the Devil, will send blackbirds to loosen it; sometimes you can hear them at work inside the coffin. And you've got to burn what's on the comb—Birdie taught me that—or else a witch will get ahold of it and scratch at that poor soul forever and a day. Lord knows, Birdie's soul deserved its rest.

A bitter storm came up out of nowhere, but we were expecting it. Everybody knows that a storm always follows an old woman's death. By morning, there was no trace of it. Oncle Joe set to making the pine box. The Judge wasn't stingy about giving us wood for coffins and saying the right words over our graves. There were some good things to him. Not many.

Eulie did all the cooking for the family, which I was

jealous about, but I had to sit with Birdie from sunup to sunup for three days. Who else would of? Isaac couldn't do it because he worked in the stable all morning and in the cotton field 'til sundown, and came home bone-achy each night. Besides, everybody knows it's bad luck to have kin tend the body.

Isaac had to dredge up the energy to dig the grave, though, along with Eulie's boy, Tom. Sure hoped Tom could stay sober through it all.

Sitting beside Birdie, I caught sight of *mon cher* Isaac's shiny-sweat back, him standing in that deep hole, tossing dirt over his shoulder like he was ridding the earth of sorrow.

After three days we laid Birdie in the ground in Oncle Joe's pine box. It was a winter's day, coldest day of my whole life, but it was blue-sky sunny; wasn't a cloud in sight that day.

Not like yesterday, rain and thunder pounding down on Lila and Sal, and all of it whipped up by that witch Eulie, to chase them off from Laurel Oaks. Has she got her own reasons, or is it just to be ornery 'cause she knows I want Lila here?

Serious as it all is, I have to chuckle. When Eulie stuffed her whole self into the skin of a cat up there in the Maude Eberly room, and Lila took down that needlepoint thing from the wall, Eulie about had a fit. Tickled me to see her clawing up there on that skinny hat rack like it was a tree!

I was hoping Lila would wave the picture around so much that the cat would fall out of that hat rack tree and crush every bone in her body, so Eulie couldn't get out ever more.

Same time, I was praying that Lila would figure out that she needed to get behind the wall where the picture hangs, to find the babies.

Saturday night. More folks are here for Camilla's sorry tour. They'll be looking in the mirror for me and poking their toes at Samuel Gladstone down by the door, but upstairs is where it counts. Lila and Gabe are upstairs now in the room where Miss Amelia's *bébés* must be wondering, what comes next? Well, don't we all wonder? My soul's throbbing like a beating heart after a foot race. Lord, what's gonna happen here? *What?*

Chapter Thirty

Lila

The hinged lid groaned as we lifted it. Inside, cradled in dark blue velvet, stood a small sculpture of two cherubs, arm-in-arm and legs entwined. They were just alike, mirror images, except one had its eyes closed.

"So, this is what Daphne meant by the babies in the wall," I said, my heart in my throat.

Gabe said, "No carcasses, too bad. I was holding out for something more weird."

"Will you settle for priceless?" The sculpture appeared to be solid gold, with ruby lips, emerald eyes, and lacy wings of ivory, or maybe white jade. Between their fat bellies and their dimpled knees, they shared a drape of thin gold mesh, layered like fish scales, and on the one big toe of each of the baby angels a heart-shaped diamond glistened. "Sheesh, this thing must be worth a hundred thousand dollars."

"Let me hold it a minute."

I passed it to Gabe. "Whoa! I wouldn't want to drop it on my foot." He turned it this way and that. "Way too adorable."

"I've seen something like this in a book," I said, trying to call up a dim memory, or impression, or was it a vision of the future? Time—past/present/future—were all muddled. My heart was thumping with the possibilities.

Gabe lifted the fish-scale drape over the cherubs, revealing some engraved words. "Can't make it out. Can you?" He squinted to read the filigreed engraving. "This looks like a C, with all kinds of curlicues snaking around it. An A, I think, and then an M . . ."

The light shifted as though a cloud were passing over the house. No, it wasn't so much a shift as a ripple in the light, a shimmery image you might get in a pond. For the flash of a second, I was sure Daphne was there!

". . . and then, maybe, a B, or it could be an E . . ."

I tapped my finger to my lips to hush Gabe so I could hear Daphne. Her unearthly, soft voice pleaded, *Watch, take care, beware,* and she slid into the light like a card sliding into the deck.

"Daphne's warning us, Gabe. We might be in danger."

His head snapped up. "Danger? Woo. I guess she'd know. The tree must have clued her in." I couldn't tell if

Gabe took me seriously, but at least he didn't roll his eyes. He went on reading the letters on the statues: C . . . A . . . M . . . B . . . R . . .

"Cambridge, of course!" I cried. "That was Judge Nethercott's wife's family. Is that what you're afraid of, Daphne? Something about the Cambridges?" I asked softly. "What else does it say, Gabe?"

"Now I've got the hang of it. A-M-E-L. Amelia Maye." He struggled to make out the other name letter by letter and finally got, "Ophelia Raye. Cute rhyme."

"Twins? Maybe Mrs. Nethercott had a twin."

"An evil twin," Gabe said with a diabolical grin. "Or maybe Amelia's the evil one." The smile vanished from his lips. "You really think Daphne's here?"

"Do you sense her?"

He looked around, as if he desperately *wanted* to see her, or somehow get proof that she was with us in the room. "No."

I touched the cherubic face of Amelia Maye. It felt warm, smooth, but when my fingers brushed across the closed eyes of the other statue, the baby felt cold and clammy, dead. "Gabe," I whispered, "I don't think Ophelia Raye was ever alive."

"Like, Amelia survived and Ophelia didn't?"

"That's my guess, or intuition, or whatever you want to call it."

"So what's it got to do with Daphne? You think she stole this, and Mrs. Nethercott found out, and that's why Daphne poisoned her? Sorry, Daphne," he said to the ceiling.

"No! That doesn't feel right," I protested, surprised to find myself so protective of Daphne. But why? She wanted us to find these babies. Maybe she thought they'd prove her innocence somehow. "Maybe she *didn't* do it, didn't poison the Nethercotts, Gabe."

"Back to square one. Who did?"

"Hey, I just remembered where I've seen something like these cherubs before."

"Where? In a book of magic spells?" Gabe asked hopefully.

"Don't laugh. In the Sears catalog! They were lawn ornaments."

"Aw, Lila, what a crushing comedown. Let's see if there's something more interesting in this treasure box." Gabe poked around in the midnight-blue velvet that lined the chest.

I saw the velvet slide a bit, and as I reached over to straighten it, a hint of powder-blue poked out. "What's this?" I cried, excitement rising in my belly. I eased a thick envelope out. The envelope said, *Please deliver to Père Jacques.* I had just enough French to guess: "It's a letter to her father."

"Lemme see." Gabe reached for the letter, but I tugged it away and unfolded the beautiful linen paper, brittle with age and monogrammed in another kind of curlicue script.

Small A, big C, small N . . . like Mom's monogrammed towels, with her maiden name bigger than our family name. ACN: "Amelia Cambridge Nethercott. It's hers!" I cried. I held the paper up under the glare of the Tiffany lamp. Squiggly lines were in ink faded to just a shade or two darker than the paper. "It's so dim, and her handwriting's hard to read, like maybe she scribbled it in a big hurry."

Gabe and I made out the first words:

Dear God, forgive me.

Suddenly something whisked the letter out of my hands, and it shot like a missile to the fireplace. Cold ash in the hearth had mysteriously begun smoldering again. I dashed over to retrieve the blue paper. "What was *that?*"

Gabe said, "Somebody sure doesn't want us to read that letter."

"And it's not Daphne. Daphne *wants* us to find this stuff." I reached into the fireplace and snapped up the letter just as the first flame leaped toward the chimney. A second later, and my hand would have been fried crisp.

Chapter Thirty-one

Daphne

Just after Birdie passed, Molly came old enough to go along with her sister to school in town for the best part of the day. Eulie kept the kitchen going, and for the first time in my life, I barely had enough work to do. Miss Amelia was so heartsick, she didn't give a mind to what I was doing, or not doing.

Those mornings I was waking up earlier and earlier to get to fixing breakfast before Eulie showed her saggy face in the house. Long as she still lived down in the quarters and only got called up for day work, I had a chance to keep my own self important to the family.

The Judge was always up before sunrise, and on that one day, Miss Amelia had rolled out of her tight little bed while the moon still hung over the place. So, I was cutting lard into flour for the breakfast biscuits, when I heard the two of them having the same old conversation about me, but with a fresh turn. I wasn't eavesdropping, no sir. I'd learned my lesson, all right. But with the girls still asleep, and Birdie gone, the house echoed. And sound carried. Besides, when you've just got one ear, it sharpens up like a hunting hound's, and you hear things normal folks might miss.

They were having one of their cold-ash arguments in the parlor. I think Miss Amelia's whole self turned cold with all the Judge's shaming her, and another little one on the way, and Birdie lying silent in the ground. Where Miss Amelia's heart used to beat there were just some hard pebbles knocking around now.

She said, "The girl can't handle kitchen chores. You put your fork into Daphne's squab last evening and saw the pink juices running out just as I did. That bird was still *raw,* Mr. Nethercott."

"She needs seasoning, Amelia, that's all."

"Needs seasoning, indeed, and so does her jambalaya! Eulie can handle the kitchen alone. I say we move her up here into the house and send that Daphne girl home."

Home to white folks meant down to the quarters; *home* meant out to the fields. My heart lurched up into my throat.

"You're being hasty, my dear." The Judge had a way of making *my dear* sound like *my aching back.*

"I want that girl out of my house!" I pictured Miss

Amelia's jaw locked tight, the pulse working at her hollow cheek.

"Think of someone else besides yourself, Amelia. Our girls are still getting over Birdie, and to send Daphne away so soon would break their young hearts."

"Just whose heart would be broken?" Miss Amelia said savagely. "You send her away tomorrow. Tomorrow I say, Mr. Nethercott."

"I will not. Our Molly has a birthday next week. She is entitled to some happiness, even if you can't seem to find any, my dear. She's quite attached to Daphne. Grant Molly that much joy, won't you, Amelia?"

I couldn't hear Miss Amelia's answer, if there was one, until she drove a loser's bargain with the Judge. "Then you'll have to sacrifice one of your field hands to my house. One past her prime, I might add. Perhaps the one they call Roweena. Daphne's nearly useless. She'll need more help with the cleaning and laundry and all, what with the new baby coming."

"What's that you say, Amelia?"

"Yes, Mr. Nethercott, I am with child again, as are a few of the women down in the quarters."

I knew she wasn't happy about it, and here I'd always thought everybody loved it when a new *bébé* came to the place.

"So, sir, we'll bring Roweena up here right away? And another thing, Eulie's boy Tom is coming into his own, and I say sell him off, him and Birdie's boy, both."

Sell *mon cher* Isaac away? Oh! Felt the color drain from my face 'til I must have looked like the belly of a hound.

"You've read the news from over in Virginia, same as I have, Mr. Nethercott, about that rebel Nat Turner who rose up against his master, he and a handful of other Negroes, and killed half a hundred of our folks. *White folks,* Clark. Time's are changing. We just can't risk having young bucks like Tom and Isaac around, with their sap rising."

"I will not let Tom go."

"Well, then, Mr. Nethercott, at least you'll grant me this much: Roweena comes in during the day, Eulie moves up to the house, and Daphne goes down."

"Roweena, if you wish, my dear, and I suppose we can find a corner for Eulie's bedroll, but Daphne stays, at least for a few weeks."

"Isaac, then?"

Trading Isaac for me! And her knowing we were sweet on each other. Miss Amelia was pickling in the brine of meanness. That poor *bébé* in her! Everybody knows that bitter blood sours a *bébé*-to-come.

"So, are we in agreement, Mr. Nethercott?"

"Isaac is a good and reliable stable hand," the Judge said, "a tireless picker, and a good fix-it man, besides. What transpires in the field and beyond these walls, Amelia, is of no concern of yours. I'll give it thought."

Then all the tears I'd never found for Birdie started sliding right out of my eyes. I let them fall into the biscuit dough I was kneading, worked them into that dough with every bit of grief and vengeance in my soul.

Chapter Thirty-two

Lila

The faded, hurried handwriting was hard to decipher, but we pieced it together and I read it aloud:

Dear God, forgive me. These are my last words, for I shall not survive the night . . .

"She must have written it the night of the poisoning," Gabe said. "Read it, quick."

. . . I never dreamed the kitchen girl would take my mad rantings seriously, and certainly not on dear Molly's birthday . . .

I stopped. "The kitchen girl—Daphne?"
Gabe shrugged. "Who knows?"

. . . on dear Molly's birthday. Oh! The torments of a jealous woman, languishing here in this swampy wasteland, and another child on the way. In a weak and grievous moment in the garden, indisposed as I was that morning, I leaned on the arm of Luke to support my frail being. Behind us, the girl picked cucumbers for the sweetened vinegar salad Mr. Nethercott enjoys. Sour as vinegar myself with the travails of morning sickness, I merely mentioned that my days would pass in greater tranquility if I could but rid my house of that wretched Daphne . . .

"The kitchen girl *isn't* Daphne. It must be Eulie," Gabe said.

. . . that wretched Daphne in whom my husband and children find such charms. As I strolled through Luke's abundant garden, the kitchen girl trailing behind, I recall saying, "Daphne is a pox on my household, and yet she remains." I suppose I spoke of poison, but not as the girl

*took it. Luke understood my meaning, I am cer-
tain, that being only that Daphne was poison to
my happiness, stealing the affection of my husband and children so effortlessly. I turned to
look back to be certain that Eulie . . .*

"Yes! I suspected it was Eulie," I crowed.
"Read the whole thing, before we jump to conclusions."

*. . . that Eulie grasped my meaning, and, Dear
God, her hateful gaze alarmed me as she promised to fix things so the Judge would expel Daphne
forever. Bile rising in my throat, I said nothing, but waved Eulie away. Now as I struggle to
write my last confession against the pain thun-
dering through me, I fear that the notion remained
in the foolish girl's head, something went awry,
and now we shall all three perish, my daughters
and myself. Before I go to my reward—or shall
it be my eternal punishment?—I must set the
record straight.*

"Eulie did it!" Gabe shouted. "Case closed."
"Not so fast. Don't you wonder why Amelia put this
letter in with her statue?"
"No. Let's sell it quick and make a killing," Gabe said.
"Very funny, since the whole thing's about murder." I
turned back to the letter. The handwriting got worse and
began slanting downhill, I guess because Amelia Nethercott was minutes away from croaking.

*With trembling hands, I shall slip this letter in
with my beautiful babies and trust Daphne to keep
her word, thus to save her own body and soul.
Somebody, someday, must learn the truth . . .*

"Which is what, exactly?" Gabe probed. "Spell it out for me, Amelia baby."

But there wasn't another word. Amelia Maye Cambridge Nethercott never finished the letter. I said, "She must have had just enough time to stick it in this box before she died."

"Okay, lemme see if I understand this. The woman planted the idea of the poisoning in Eulie's head?"

"She meant to get somebody sick, not dead, and frame Daphne," I speculated.

"Yeah, so Eulie actually did the nasty deed, but it backfired, and bottom line, Amelia killed her own kids. That's pretty wicked."

I waved the letter under Gabe's nose. "Now I'm thinking Daphne wanted us to find the cherubs to clear her name, but how would she know what was in the letter? I'm betting she never had a chance to learn to read."

Gabe reflected a moment. "Or maybe she didn't even know why we had to find the box, just that we did."

"And who *didn't* want us to find this letter?"

"Eulie. Obvious, isn't it?" Gabe said.

"She must have known Amelia pinned the rap on her."

"How would she know that? She probably didn't read, either."

I wished he hadn't pointed that out. Made me feel idiotic, so I tried to cover. "Maybe Amelia accused Eulie on her deathbed. Sal says Eulie's the cracked face I saw in the mirror and the one who hid the sampler from us. It all makes perfect sense now."

"Yeah, if you believe ghosts can do stuff like that," Gabe reasoned. "Of course, it could have been that Luke guy who was trotting Amelia Maye around the garden."

I scanned her words again. " 'Luke's abundant garden—' Sal said the gardener's name was Luke. He's the one who lives, lived in that shack in the field with all those gardening tools."

"Your vanishing raker dude. You think he poisoned the Nethercotts?" Gabe answered his own question: "Nah. If he blew his top, he'd just kill a bunch of plants. I'm keeping my money on Eulie."

"She's definitely our best suspect, poisoning the children and making it look like Daphne did it, to wheedle her way into Amelia Maye's good graces."

"Sure, but don't you think killing Amelia and her daughters kind of ruined Eulie's reputation with the Nethercott family?" Gabe muttered.

"You're right. We're still missing a huge chunk of the puzzle."

Gabe blew feather dust off the shrunken rooster head. "Hey, did you stop to think about how we heard a rooster crowing behind the wall, when this sucker's been dead for, like, two centuries?"

"Really strange," I agreed, lying on the floor with my

feet propped up on the bed. "You suppose Eulie had any-thing to do with the rooster business, like it was a charm or a curse, and she's the one who made this letter fly into the fire?"

"Watch out. She's out to nail us now that she knows *we* know she's the villain."

I clutched the letter, so Eulie's spirit could not snatch it away from me again. Our eyes darted into every corner of the room, waiting for Eulie to strike.

Chapter Thirty-three

Daphne

That day, the oleander day, Isaac came up to the house to give the Judge a letter from the post. Passed by the kitchen window and said, "Psst!" when Eulie was busy wiping up some spilt flour in the larder. I ran outside to talk to *mon cher* behind the kitchen, my heart beating like a drum, maybe because I was scared, or maybe just crazy with love for that beautiful boy, dark as the walnut shelves in the Judge's library.

He said, "You learn much about healing from Mama Birdie?"

"Maybe." I was ashamed to tell him how little I'd picked up from her.

Eulie stuck her head out the window. "What you two doing out there? Boy, git away before the Judge whup you good!" She grumbled something about no-account stable boys, and how he'd be long gone in a day or two anyway, and good riddance.

"Best have some healing skills," Isaac said.

Healing what? I wondered. Had somebody taken sick? Was it about something he'd learned from his *maman*? Or something he'd heard other folks bragging about? Before I could ask him a thing, he loped away like a fine stag.

Later that day, out picking mint for Miss Amelia's fruit tea, I couldn't help stumbling over Luke Mullin. Shaded by his big white floppy hat, like a gentleman gardener, you couldn't tell that he was bald as a peeled potato. Folks said he shaved off his hair to show he was high-born, just like he talked proper to let us know he was born and bred a free Yankee. A lot of good it did him, hanging around here at Laurel Oaks.

"Um hmmn," he said, all gravelly voiced, since he hardly talked to anybody day in and day out. "That's a good patch of mint, nice and sweet."

I snapped off a few leaves and held them to my nose. Ahh! Stuck a twig over my good ear so I could smell of it all the day long.

Luke Mullin never talked to a person direct, and especially not to me. He talked to a fly flitting by or a hanging vine or a vegetable, but you always knew whose ears his fancy words were meant for.

"Um hmmn," he said, "I'm just pondering why that fellow you fancy was out here picking flowers this morning before the sun was even high in the sky."

"Isaac?" I asked, picturing a fancy bunch of posies he'd be handing me through the kitchen window when Eulie went to the necessary or some such.

"Is that the boy's name?" he asked a smashed tomato.

"Oh, Luke Mullin, who you fooling? You know everybody on this plantation!"

"Um hmmn. Isaac was picking a bouquet for a young lady, I reckon."

"That rascal," I said, feeling my cheeks flame up.

"I had to tell him which ones to watch out for, which ones have the poison in them." He tossed a handful of weeds into a bucket, then peered in like he could see his stubbly face reflected in it. "What's the name of that grouchy kitchen gal?"

"Eulie?" Even saying the name left a bitter spark on my tongue.

"Um hmmn, that one. She was out here picking flowers today, too. You're just about the only one not stripping my flowerbeds, Miss Daphne."

I swear, the man blushed when he spoke out my name. Birdie always used to say, "Isaac, watch out for that Luke Mullin man. Be sure he ain't come picking Daphne like a summer flower!"

Luke Mullin cleared his froggy throat. "That mint's sweet as a baby's breath." Suddenly he looked right at me, doing his best to pull his eyes straight forward. "I reckon you know which flowers have the poison in them, don't you?"

I glanced over at the dogbane, the foxglove, the oleander that grew wild on the outside of Luke Mullin's vegetable garden. Birdie'd tried to teach me all about them, but I could have picked one for the bright color, or the pretty shape of the leaf, and never *think* about its poison whammy.

"That Eulie, you reckon she knows?"

"Everything she touches turns to poison," I muttered.

"Um hmmn. Watch her, Miss Daphne. She's a wily one, that gal."

Didn't I know it!

Then Luke Mullin said, "Over yonder, that pink, it's fennel. Gives you seeds good for the gullet. And this one's figwort. Clears out the pipes in a person's body."

"Why are you talking about this, Luke Mullin?" Like Isaac was, just a bit ago.

He shrugged, and his hat flopped around his shoulders. "Just in case someone up at the house gets poorly. Accidentally," he added, studying a tangle of wriggly worms in his compost heap. "No special reason."

I said I'd remember—about as long as it took me to get back to the house.

I waited that whole day long for *mon cher* Isaac to bring me those flowers he'd picked, but he never did. I even went out to the stable in case he was too shy to come up to the house. He wasn't there, though, so I guess Candlewax sniffed the bunch of flowers in my place.

That whole day, Eulie never gave me a minute's peace while we cooked for my Molly's birthday party. We made her favorites, crawfish gumbo, and beefsteak rolled up in goose liver paste, baked up in a crinkly-crusty dough. I declare, it took us forty hours to fix it and left us hardly a minute to make the three-layer butter crunch birthday gâteau she was partial to. Don't know what all went into that cake, we whipped it up so fast. A pinch of nutmeg, a sprinkle or two of cinnamon, a handful of sugar, nine eggs, because we always did things in nines for good luck, same as a novena, and we beat those fat hens' eggs up all frothy. The cake barely had time to cool before we iced it thick and set it back on the wide-open windowsill a short while before we took it to the table for the family.

Shouldn't of.

Anybody could have sprinkled dried up oleander leaves on that cake, or worked a few drops of sap into the fluffy yellow icing. Eulie, maybe, or, good Lord, even *mon cher* Isaac. Or I could have put something in it, not meaning to. We had field mice that got into the pantry. Could have been a mouse burrowing into the flour sack before he gave up and died of the oleander rat poison we set out, just like Birdie taught me.

And it's me scooped up the flour for the cake, not Eulie.

Chapter Thirty-four

Lila

I whispered, "Do you think Eulie knows we're looking for her, Gabe?"

"You're asking *me* what ghosts know? I don't know if they're spying on you every minute, or if they even exist."

"Gabe! How can you doubt at this point?" I waved the letter at him again. "And think of that dried up rooster. You heard it crowing, and it's been dead a couple of centuries."

He sighed. "Maybe I'm nuts, too."

"Oh!" I wasn't responding to his words, but to a weird

change in the room. Call it a drop in barometric pressure, or a rise, or maybe it's more like having the air sucked out of the space you're in, but suddenly the room felt profoundly quiet, and only then did I realize how it had buzzed with untolled presences earlier. "I think Eulie's gone."

"Where?"

"I don't know where! To wherever ghosts go when they're off duty."

"Like the school bus barn," Gabe said. "Maybe all the ghosts hang out together somewhere until they get called to the front lines. The National Guard of Ghouls."

I thought about Sal telling us that some ghosts were restless because they had unfinished business to take care of.

Gabe and I were on the same wavelength, because he said, "Gimme just a minute, and I'll make sense of the whole mess." He stared at the empty hole in the wall, as if he were reading the answers off a chalkboard, then at the cherubs, and then he scanned the letter again. "Theory: suppose Eulie's been wallowing in guilt all these one hundred and seventy years for murdering the Nethercotts. She's dragging around a double dose of guilt because Daphne's gotten the bum rap for it. Follow me so far?"

"It's not that hard, Gabe. Okay, so now that the truth is out, she's free to retire to Florida like Gram and Gramps."

"Is that in her contract? Or are ghosts always hanging around, looking for action?" Gabe joked, but I sensed that he was jittery about it all, like me. In fact, we were both giddy—with roller-coaster-type fear one minute, worry about Mom and Dad the next; total clear awareness one minute, then nagging doubt right after that.

Gabe said, "I guess it's all over for Eulie, and she doesn't have to haul the guilt around anymore like a sack of rocks."

"Amelia Maye must have been a loony bird!" I sucked in my belly until it was concave enough to hold a basketball. "See? Wearing those torturous corsets will do that to you. Can't tell what you'd do if you were all trussed up like Amelia Maye Nethercott."

Silence, as if we were actually contemplating a life with our intestines pushed up around our ears.

Then Gabe said, "I have just one little question bugging me. What's the tree got to do with the whole thing?"

I shook my head in confusion. "Maybe Sal knows something, but she doesn't want to tell us. She does seem to be a little evasive about the tree, even though she led me right to it. Almost like she was saying, there's something there, but I don't want to know what. You think she's afraid of the spirits around here?"

"Should she be?" Gabe asked. "Should we be? Okay, Lila, if you're sure that tree communicates with you—I mean, I'm not exactly buying it—but if it does, I want to know what it has to say, and I want to hear it right from the horse's mouth."

I threw the curtain open to see the tree, then remembered that my room faced the back of the house, and Daphne's tree was out front. Beautiful sunshine streamed in through the window. The statue's gold and diamonds glistened in the warm rays.

"These cherubs, that's what we have to focus on, Gabe, not that dried-up rooster head in the ashtray or vengeful ghosts or poisoned kids." I unlocked the window and slid it open, inhaling the goopy Louisiana air.

"You're letting out the air-conditioning," Gabe grumbled.

"Hush." I put my palm out behind me in a *hold it* position. "I'm watching that irritating cat scratch her way up the tree outside this window."

She lazily settled on a branch to take a nap in the sunshine, then spotted me. Yellow eyes glared back at me, those knowing-almost-human eyes. I tilted my head to see her more clearly. She let out a banshee wail as she stretched her front legs and scratched at the loose bark.

"Ow," I said, rubbing my arm, not sure whether I was feeling the pull on the cat's own claws, or the pain of the oak harboring that cat.

Eulie. The name wrote itself on the inside of my eyelids as those yellow eyes bored into my own. Was the cat really Eulie's spirit? Couldn't be! And yet . . .

"I don't think we've heard the last from Eulie," I whispered.

The cat began to chase her tail in a frantic effort to settle on a branch, as though she were an unwelcome guest in a hostile tree. Right, like trees decide who's going to climb them or not. And then, as if *Eulie* were erased, a new name came into my head.

"Timberlarken," I said.

"Who?"

"It's somebody's name, Timberlarken."

"The cat's?" asked Gabe.

"I don't know." My words seemed remote, as though muffled by clothes in a closet. "Timberlarken, Timberlarken." I rolled the word around on my tongue. "Larken, lark, some kind of small bird. And timber. It's what you build houses with."

"Or what you shout in the forest when some ax man whacks a tree. Tim-BERRRR!!!" Gabe shouted.

Suddenly, with my eyes fixed on the cat, it came clear to me what—no, *who*—Timberlarken was. "Daphne's tree!"

"The Ear Tree? The tree has a *name*? Give me a break, Lila."

"It does, yes! And we've got to go out there right now!"

"Okay, but I'm taking my baseball bat just in case one of the ghosts pulls a fast one." Gabe yanked me to my feet. "Gotta hustle and get this business done before Mom and Dad get back, or we're in major trouble. They wouldn't be too thrilled to see their offspring in meaningful dialogue with vegetable life."

Chapter Thirty-five

Daphne

All of them sat down at the table, the Judge and Miss Amelia at the head and foot, with about ten fat candles glowing up and down the table, and Alice and Molly crosswise to them.

Eulie was nervous as a tree squirrel getting out the gumbo speckled with parsley that the Judge favored. It'd be sloshing with good stuff, by Birdie's recipe, but Eulie's soup was thick enough to shovel up, and too peppery. The Judge took two bites and let his spoon drop to the table. He made his opinions known, that man. Miss Amelia just took dainty dabs at her coated spoon. Hardly ate anything on a good day, but now, big with child, her stomach was more finicky than usual.

Molly, having her seventh birthday that night, was just too churned up to sit still. She fiddled so much that she tumbled right off her chair.

"Compose yourself, Molly," Miss Amelia said as I scooped the child up off the floor. I had to press her shoulder to keep her fixed in place, while I shooed flies, cranking a big red feather fan.

"Oh, mercy be," Alice said, rolling her eyes toward the ceiling. At nine, she thought she was some fine young lady, fixing to start rouging up her cheeks and shucking off her pinafores for fitted frocks. I never saw the girl look prettier than she did that night, all fancied up in a sky-blue dress with a sash two shades darker. Had on silk stockings that night, too. I know that because I had to peel them off her later when she got so sick.

The Judge made a big show of looking all over the table. "I don't see any raspberry jam, do you, my dear? I thought it was known in the kitchen that I like a spread of raspberry jam on my bread."

Eulie ran to fetch the jam. Took her a long time, too, because I'd hidden it back of the burlap potato sack in the larder. I snickered behind my hand, picturing her tearing the kitchen apart to find that little glass cup of jam!

While she was hunting it down I looked from one to the other of these fine-dressed folks, and even now, that's how I remember them clearest—that night in the candlelight, the Judge crunching through the pastry crust around the beefsteak, Alice picking bits of bacon out of the col-

lard greens, and Molly looking over her shoulder for the
birthday cake she knew'd be coming, with eight candles
burning, one for good luck.

The good luck one didn't work, that's a fact.

"Done to perfection," the Judge said, finishing his last
bite of beefsteak, and Eulie beamed shamelessly. I noticed
her cheeks were feverish like she was real excited about
something besides that beef and goose liver mess.

"Eulie's coming along," Miss Amelia said. "But she's
not Birdie. I suppose even Daphne had her hand in this
meal," Miss Amelia said, puffing out a weary sigh. She
said my name like it had barbs in it, even though she gave
me that name herself, after the Greeks' story.

As usual, the Judge and Miss Amelia talked about us
like we weren't there. Now, how's it possible we were so
invisible, since we were huffing back and forth to the
kitchen to tend to them every minute?

"Mama?" Alice said, "I am just so tired of reading the
same books over and over. Can't we go to the lending
library in town first thing tomorrow?"

Miss Amelia's mornings were rocky with the *bébé* fixing to pip, so she said, "We'll see if Isaac can ride us in tomorrow afternoon, before your father sends him away."

Isaac! My heart leaped up, and what popped into my
head was the flowers he never gave me. Must be waiting
until after supper, I thought, to woo me in the moonlight.

Molly squirmed like a shrimp on the deck of a boat.
"Alice got a Shetland for her seventh. I'm just reminding
you, in case you forgot. Isaac says there's room in the
stable for my pony. Don't send him off. We need Isaac to

tend *my* pony, Daddy. A bay, reddish-brown like your hair. Please? Please?"

"After we have your birthday cake we'll talk about presents," Miss Amelia said, tinkling her little call-us bell. "Eulie, I believe you have a cake set by out there?"

"Yes'm," Eulie yelled from the serving pantry.

She marched in with that downhill cake, puddling yellow icing off the side and the candle wax melting all over it. Molly loved it, since everything she did was a little lopsided anyway. She dipped right into the icing and sucked it off her finger, until Miss Amelia gave her a glare that would melt ice.

The Judge took one look at the whole calamity of the cake and busted out laughing, and that's when Eulie folded her arms across her jiggly chest and said to Miss Amelia, "Daphne done the cake her whole self."

Chapter Thirty-six

Lila

The sun hid in oaks taller even than Daphne's tree.

"Sure this is the right tree?" Gabe asked. "They all kind of look alike."

"Only one way to prove it." I shone a flashlight up through the lacy shade of leaves.

"Yeah," Gabe conceded, "and the ear thing sure looks freaky in that light."

I dropped the flashlight to the ground. "The light's too harsh for the tree."

"It told you that?" Gabe asked.

"It wants us to do this in natural light—sun and shade and shadow."

"Except for that light from the second floor of the house," Gabe reminded me. "Let the light go out, and the spirits will be released. Oooooooh!"

"Get serious, Gabe, or I'm doing this whole thing without you."

"Right." He cleared his throat and stood ramrod-straight, with the baseball bat slung over his right shoulder.

The Ear Tree loomed above us, with its deep brown arms gracefully reaching for the sky. Its leaves billowed in the gentle afternoon breeze. Its bark, like leathery winter skin, welcomed my sweaty touch. I sensed all this but had no idea how I knew it.

Gabe's voice shattered the stillness. "What's our game plan?"

"I don't exactly have one. Yet. Quiet, so we can hear it. Him. The tree."

That strange word wrote itself in my mind again. I silently repeated it like one of Mom's yoga mantras. Timberlarken. Timberlarken.

Gabe inched his way close to me and spoke softly. "We have to have a plan, Lila. Too important to just wing it."

"Okay, here's a plan, sort of. You squirrel up the tree like you did last night. You'll just be a kind of lookout. If it makes you nervous, just suck it up." I pointed to a wide, reliable branch about a third of the way up the tree. "That one will hold you. I'll hand the baseball bat up to you. Then I'll back up against the trunk."

The Secret of Laurel Oaks   219

"The tree's message will come to you through your butt?"

"Gabriel, please!"

He took a deep breath and began scaling the tree trunk until one sneaker landed on a weak branch, which broke off and fell to the ground at my feet. "Oh, man, close one!" Gabe hollered.

But it wasn't his fear I was in touch with just then. It was the seering throb in my own arm for a few seconds. *The tree's pain from the broken branch?*

Just then, Sal's school bus pulled up, at least two hours early. In a minute, she came skipping up the driveway. When she noticed me, she said, "Back at the tree? I might've known." She stepped way back. "Hey, lucky thing happened today. Water pipes broke at that no-good schoolhouse Miss Camilla sends me to. Everybody got to go home, if you call this home. Now I can get me a orange Popsicle and catch *I Love Lucy* on the *tee*-vee." She seemed to make a wide circle of the tree, like she was nervous about being pulled into its orbit.

"Camilla won't know you're home yet, and Gabe and I need your help, Sal."

Gabe rattled some twigs and leaves, and Sal looked up. "I'm the ape in the tree," he said, making some *chee-chee* monkey sounds.

"What're you doing up there, Yankee boy? What's he got that baseball bat for? Can't whack a ghost."

I pulled her closer to the tree. "Sal? Does Timberlarken talk to you?"

"Who's that?"

"You know!"

"I don't neither, and now *Lucy*'s half over, and I ain't had a lick of the Popsicle."

"You're not a ghost, are you?" Ridiculous thought, but I had to ask.

She threw up her arms at the absurdity of the question and snapped, "If I was a ghost, you think I'd hang with Miss Camilla? No sir, I'd find me better places to haunt. A baseball park, or the Ice Capades, not this run-down bundle of boards."

We were used to the cheery, mischievous Sal. This one, with her angry sparks, surprised me.

She pouted and stuck her nose in the air. "So, you go talk to that tree like he's your last best friend in the whole parish." She turned her back to me and squared her shoulders. The sight of those determined shoulders on her small frame nearly brought tears to my eyes. She huffed and sighed, but she didn't walk away.

Suddenly it dawned on me. "The tree doesn't communicate with you, does it, Sal?"

She shot the answer over her shoulder: "Course not. You thinkin' I'm a loony bird, like you?"

"But you told me if I knew how to listen—"

"Guess I don't," she said petulantly.

"And it makes you sad that you can't hear the tree's voice." I put my arm around her. "I'm sorry. Please stay and help us. Maybe you'll hear him."

Gabe called down from his perch, "My sister's going

to make you miserable if you don't do what she says. I've lived with her for thirteen years. I know. See? She chased me up this tree, and I don't like being anywhere higher than a refrigerator."

"Pitiful, that's what you are, Yankee boy." She flipped around with a look full of all kinds of things I couldn't read. A sigh came all the way from her toes, and her shoulders fell. "Aw, hell's bells, *Lucy*'s 'bout over now, and Miss Camilla has got those Popsicles counted like they're chunks of gold. Can't barely sneak one past her eyeballs."

I smiled. "Come here, Sal." Reluctantly, she took my hand. "I'm going to stand with my back to the tree and my arms stretched out. You do the same. I want us to make a circle around the tree, until our hands touch."

"What for, anyway?"

"It just feels right, somehow. Trust me."

"I don't trust anybody." Still, she followed my directions and stretched her arms around her half of the tree trunk. "Not gonna do anything but pull our arms out of their sockets," she muttered, with her voice shaking a little.

"You scared, Sal?" I called behind me.

"Me? Scared? I ain't scared of nothing. Just this tree, it ain't natural, a tree picking somebody to tell its secrets to." She paused. "And that somebody ain't me."

I remembered Sal telling me her grandmother had said, once you give a thing a name, it belongs to you. "The tree's name is Timberlarken, Sal. Say it, Timberlarken."

I couldn't hear; she might have whispered his name.

I felt his rough bark on my back through my T-shirt,

and I sensed his impatience. "Come on, Sal, put your hands in mine." We clasped hands, with our feet planted firmly as if they could root, and our arms stretched behind us as far as possible. Minutes ticked by, with only crickets to keep time. My shoulders ached.

"Anything happening down there?" Gabe called.

Sal muttered, "What're you expecting? Timberlarken, my *behind*."

"Be patient, both of you!" I tilted my head back. My heart rate slowed as my eyes adjusted to the golden shade of the thick leaf growth. But even the shade had varying levels of darkness, and now I started seeing patches faintly gray and shimmery, like digital pictures clearing up on the computer screen. No identifiable shapes or even outlines distinguished them from anything else, but I sensed definite disturbances in the atmosphere, random rips in the fabric of the afternoon.

"Be very quiet," I whispered to Sal. "I don't want you to miss anything."

"*The Jeffersons* come on after *Lucy*. What I'm missing's good *tee*-vee."

Gabe shifted around. "My butt's getting numb."

"Sit still up there for heaven's sake. And Sal, whatever you do, don't let go. Hold on and listen, just listen."

"We're expecting a botanical data dump," Gabe said from way up in the tree.

"Don't mind how disrespectful my brother is. Quiet. Think of this like we're in church."

"Hallelujah and amen," Sal said. Then, "Okay, okay, I'm listening."

Chapter Thirty-seven
Daphne

I'm looking at Lila and Sal over there, backs smashed up against Timberlarken's trunk, standing still like they're trees their own selves. Something's happening—look at Lila's face. He's telling them all about it, maybe telling them things I don't even know from that day when he was my worst enemy and my best friend, both.

The pain of it washes through me all over again—me stretching my toes, but it's too far to touch ground, and the harder I try to reach, the tighter the rope pulls. That's where it always stops. "Birdie!" I howl. "Tante Drucilla!"

Both gone. The whole scene of that day plays in my

mind slow, like it's being pulled through a strong river current. Same as the oleander night, both rememories soaked in dread.

I watch them cutting into the birthday cake, and Molly's face is a shining moon, while she's waiting to sink her fork into that gâteau. Alice is trying to be grown up, but her eyes are gleaming, too, because who can pass up a big wedge of yellow cake oozing out with icing? I keep eyeing that cake greedily, hoping they won't finish it all so I can have a mouthful when it goes back to the kitchen—which I never got to do because of what happened after dinner.

A little white mongrel clicks by on the hardwood edge around Miss Amelia's rug from Philadelphia. Makes my head spin, because there's never been a house dog in the family. Nobody but me hears him or sees him, and I hold my tongue so I don't scare my girls.

Miss Amelia says, "Mr. Nethercott? How is your sweet tooth tonight?" She starts to slide a piece of cake onto one of those blue and white plates she favors, but the Judge had already passed judgment on the cake when Eulie brought it to the table, and he waves the slice away as if the very sight of it irks his prickly tongue. I see Molly's face fall. *What? My daddy won't even taste my birthday cake?*

Miss Amelia doesn't want a bite of it, I can tell, on account of her jumpy stomach, but she cuts herself a slim, no-thank-you sliver and takes up her fork.

Ever wish you could stop time? Just stick your foot in the cog of the wheel and stop it rolling? Sure do now, looking back on it. But the wagon kept rumbling on.

All three ladies lift the first forkful of cake into their mouths. That's all it takes, one forkful.

Eulie and I hear the talking from the serving pantry. It's Alice who says, "Y'all think the cake tastes funny?"

"Scrumptious," Molly says, scraping icing off with her teeth.

Even now, after all these years, I cringe at the echoey sound of that fork scrinching across my Molly's teeth.

Alice lets her fork clatter to her plate. "Well, I think it has an odd undertaste."

"A pinch too much baking soda," says Miss Amelia.

"Birdie's cake never tasted like this," Alice says. "And I don't believe for a minute that Daphne made it. It's bitter, like Eulie."

Eulie glances at me, and something flickers in her eyes. Fear? She hurries into the dining room, me right behind her, and whips those cake plates out from under the ladies' forks.

"Musta picked up something from the air," she says. "I'll make you a new cake tomorrow, a three-stack choc'lit. You'll like that, Miss Molly."

"I want *this* cake," Molly says, pounding the table.

Miss Amelia's face is fixed hard as glass. "Eulie's cake will be even better than Daphne's." She glares at me like she's won whatever battle we've been fighting.

That bothery little white mutt turns eyes like black-eyed peas toward me. Makes me think of what Birdie warned me once: "Mongrel like that gonna walk through the wall and vanish like steam off a soup kettle, and then you know somebody gonna die before dawn come."

I quick close the dining-room door, and the kitchen door for double sure, but when I come back in to where the family's sitting, the white dog's gone, just like Birdie said. Molly clutches her stomach. "Oh, Mama, I've got such a cramp!" she wails, and in a minute, all three of them are doubled over with the pain.

Everything starts whirling in that house, like a big dandelion in the wind. Alice and Molly sink to the floor, clutching their bellies, and Miss Amelia turns the color of bread flour, frothing at the mouth, no different from a hound foaming rabies spit.

The Judge carries her upstairs, saying, "Come with me, Daphne," but I want to stay with my girls. "Daphne," he says sharply, so what could I do? I help her out of her clothes and barely get her to the chamber pot, and you know how it goes, after all the Judge and I had been through, it shames me to be there with him, Miss Amelia in her unders, so undignified.

She shivers with the chills, teeth clattering. When she catches her breath, she croaks out a few words: "Everything's blurry. I can't see straight, Clark."

I've nearly never heard her call that man by his given name; always Mr. Nethercott, or the Judge.

She's clutching her rosaries and mumbling over each bead. Then she blinks and widens her eyes, like when you're trying to see underwater, and focuses on my face. "Get . . . her out . . . of here!"

"My dear, you need a girl's help," the Judge says, settling her back on the bed.

"Eulie. Not . . . this one. I must talk to Eulie."

The pitiful woman reaches up and yanks on the Judge's vest, pulling him down until his nose nearly pokes hers. "Daphne . . . poisoned . . . my children, Clark. She did."

"I did no such, ma'am. I swear it!" How could she lie about me that way?

The Judge rears up and turns a look of pure venom on my face. And then it rattles my bones to wonder, could I of done it and not know?

He grabs ahold of my arm in a killing grip and jerks me out of the room. My feet clunk every step as he drags me down by the hair. Drops me on the floor at the bottom, stomping my leg once to be sure I'm down for good. Where he'd had my arm, all the blood has drained away, and his cigar fingers are branded into my skin with four streaks of cool white flame.

I hear weeping and wailing—Eulie. There's a useless fool if ever there was one. Folks have been called up from the quarters—Roweena and Tante Drucilla to pick up the dining room and set the kitchen right, Isaac to bring back Doc Ramsey first, then Père Jacques, but that could take half the night. Even Luke Mullin's come up from his shed way out back. I barely catch a shadow of him and Tom, each of them carrying one of my girls up the back stairs. Therese's sent to clean up the messes those three sick ones are making, and all of them step over me lying on the floor at the foot of the stairs. Have to pick myself up.

Have to remember what Birdie did about healing bad stomachs. If it was poison had them all down, why I'd have to . . . what? Can't think of a thing, not a thing. Chills, fever—red pepper tea? Pomegranate seeds and crushed mint? Which one works for stomachache? Tea from the leaves of the peach tree, or is it calamus root? Catnip, tobacco, turpentine? Sassafras or mullein? Can't remember a thing Birdie taught me, or anything Luke said, neither.

But I can comfort my girls 'til Doc Ramsey gets here, so I stumble to my feet. The Judge's boot bruised my ankle, the one with Isaac's string around it; that swollen foot can barely hold me up. I half crawl, half drag myself up the stairs to Molly's room first. Take one look at her, lying there with her eyes sunken and ringed in black, her hands limp hanging over the side of the bed, and I fear the worst.

"Molly?" I stroke her fevered cheeks.

She looks at me like she's never seen me before. Says, "Fish fastened tight on the hook?"

Saying nonsense. "Don't talk, *bébé*."

She draws her knees up to her belly. "Hurts," she moans. "Hurts so bad. I want my mama."

"Your *maman's* feeling a little puny right now. Here, let me help you." I wet a cloth and wash her hot little face.

She gapes her mouth open, starts flailing her arms, stares up into my face with those sunken red eyes. Says, "Who are you?"

"Daphne. You know Daphne, *bébé*."

"Mama," she shouts. "Daddy!" You can be sure I scoot out of that room as soon as the Judge comes running in. Can't afford any more broken or bruised parts, with everybody needing me upstairs.

I peek into Miss Amelia's room. She's alone, down on the floor, feeling around under her bed. The only thing under there is the little chest with her *bébés* in it.

"Ma'am? I can get it for you."

She sits back with her bloomers flumed out around her, glaring at me real mean, but I fetch it anyway and tuck it out of sight, under her covers. Her hair's all undone, wild as a lion's mane. Says, "Get me my monogrammed blue stationery, and my ink pen, and remember your promise to me. After that, I never, ever want to see your hateful face again, hear?"

I do what she says. Take a minute anyway to settle her back in her bed. Her silk skin that never saw the sun is dry and flaky as raw oats. "Doctor be here soon," I whisper, and slip out of that room.

Open Alice's door and find Eulie in there, trying to comb Alice's gnarly hair, and the child fighting her like a wolf.

"What's it matter if her hair's combed? Let the poor girl be."

"You done this," Eulie hisses. "What you put in that cake?"

"Me? You!"

"Hush up, both of you," Alice moans. She laces her hands over the top of her head, like it might explode if she doesn't hold it together.

There's a commotion in the hall. The Judge is having it out with Tom and Luke Mullin. Eulie gets real nervous about hearing her boy come under the lash of the Judge's tongue. She flies out into the hall, and I'm left with my Alice.

"Daphne?" She takes my hand and kneads it for bread dough. Such a firm grip with those piano-playing fingers, and that gives me hope, until she says, "I hope the priest gets here in time for last rites. Pray for my eternal soul, Daphne," and she lets go of my hand and closes her eyes, and such a peace comes over her that I can't do a thing but smile at that beautiful child, gone to a better place than this cruel world.

Out in the hall, my eyes catch one of Luke Mullin's wandering ones, and he moves in close to me, like a watch-dog when I tell the Judge that his daughter's passed.

What does the Judge do in his grief? He takes it out on Tom. Hurls that boy down the stairs, with Eulie scrambling after him to pick up the pieces. But Tom is as sturdy as a bull, and there aren't any pieces to collect. Luke Mullin gives him a hand up, and the two of them walk out the door. Shut it nice and gentle.

That night all three passed—Alice, Molly, and Miss Amelia—before Doc Ramsey or Père Jacques, either one, ever got to the house, and I saw something I never thought my tired eyes would spy. The Judge crying. His whole body shaking. And the caterwauls that came out of that man were what you'd hear with the first jab of the knife into a fine hog. Served him right, but even hating him so, it would of broken my heart if it wasn't already cracked into a hundred pieces over my Molly and my Alice.

Chapter Thirty-eight

Lila

"Shh!" I squeezed both Sal's hands and listened even more intensely. Strange thoughts I didn't even know were stored in my head flooded me now.

About another tree that spoke to a human. No, not a tree, a lowly bush. Sunday school, Exodus. Moses standing before the Burning Bush, and the Voice saying, "Remove thy sandals from thy feet, for the place on which thee stands is holy ground."

I gently kicked off my sandals and let the soft padding of my foot probe the base of the tree where it met the warm earth from which it had sprung.

And stories I had no memory of ever hearing before,

stories populated by Africans, played through my mind like fast-forwarded videos. *A girl sinks into mud and disappears, wailing, "The ghosts have taken me! The ghosts!" The priest demands sacrifices at this sacred spot, and here a tree begins to grow out of the muddy grave of the girl . . . A woman weeps at her mother's gravesite, when the earth parts and a stalk sprouts and grows rapidly into a sapling, then a tree lucious with fruit. Its leaves rustling in the wind tell the woman that her mother's spirit hovers near, and that to speak with her mother, she must reach for the fruit of the tree, which it gently bends toward her . . .*

"Yipes! What was that?" Sal cried. "Bet it's that cat!"

A second later it flitted across my foot, jarring me out of my daydream. Now I could make out two luminous marbles—yellow eyes. She scurried up the tree to a branch just above me with her loathsome tail hanging down and brushing the top of my head. I ducked; the tail followed, making sure I knew she was there. Establishing her territory? Threatening? Or maybe she was jealous, as if to say, *Why won't the tree talk to me, too?*

It wouldn't. I felt sure that Timberlarken spoke to no other spirit but Daphne's.

We waited—for what?

"My arms are about to fall off," Sal grumbled.

"Mine, too. Shh." My shoulders were killing me, and I needed to scratch my cheek where the mosquitoes were having an afternoon snack. I tried blowing the bugs away each time one lit on my arms or my face, reminding myself, *Don't let go!* It was crucial that we maintain our sacred

circle around the tree. I leaned my head back and watched
a few sparkly dots of sunshine twinkling through the
jungle of branches against the sky. The cat's tail thumped
my head, then she scampered down a few branches and
landed with a whomp on the ground, yellow intelligent
eyes almost begging me to grasp something she knew. I
blinked, and in that flash-second, the cat shimmered into
a large dark shadow and disappeared among the statues.
Suddenly the shadows grew denser.

"Oh, man, bad news!" Gabe called. "The light on the
second floor just winked out. They warned us, remember?
When the light goes out, the spirits are released?"

Sal squeezed my hand. "Doesn't have to be bad news,
Yankee boy. Could mean released outta their pity-poor
lives, not set loose to spook us." She started to pull her
hand away.

"Don't let go; don't let go! Gabe, what do you see from
up there?"

"Nothing. The whole house is thrown into shadow, as
if it's just erasing, disappearing from film. I'd swear I'm
looking at the place before it was completely built. Too
strange. I'm coming down."

"Wait, something's happening."

Gabe froze on a high branch, waiting for a signal.

I felt myself melting into the tree. I could hear, could
feel sap running as though it were in my own veins, thrumming in my own ears. For the first time I understood what
Mr. Blakley, my life science teacher, always said: "Remember, ladies and gents, plants and trees aren't just nature's

wallpaper. They're alive. They breathe and eat and grow and die, just like we do."

Yes, this tree was definitely pulsing with life, harboring images and feelings. I listened as I'd never listened to anything or anyone before, from deep, deep within my mind.

I tapped Sal's thumb, but didn't break our concentration by speaking. Like early in the morning, under the spell of a captivating dream, and if I murmur a single word, the dream—even its memory trace—vanishes forever.

I held my breath and whispered, finally, "The tree welcomes us, Sal. Because we know the truth about Daphne. That she didn't murder those children. The tree's always known, but no one's listened to it before us."

"I always knew," Sal said quietly.

The cat mewled, demanding attention again. Sal asked, "My grandmama's right—that's you in there, ain't it, Eulie?"

We heard a hissing response from behind a bush.

"Forget the cat. Just listen!" I told the others. We let the silence surround us for a few minutes. I breathed shallowly so as not to miss a single word from Timberlarken. "He says . . . he says . . . Omigod, they hanged Daphne from this tree!"

Sal's hand jerked. "Who did? That judge?"

I shook my head against the punishing bark. "Other slaves. Her enemies."

"I'm definitely coming down."

I heard Gabe shimmy down the tree trunk, then thump to the ground as the cat had.

Tears welled up in my eyes as I recounted the message: "It was bright daylight when they hanged her, but as
shady-dark as it is now when someone cut her down. One
man, like a brother or a boyfriend."

"To bury her?" Gabe asked.

"She wasn't never buried," Sal said, and I heard her
voice clotted with tears.

"Yes. Others came . . . they took her away."

"Keep it coming," Gabe whispered beside me.

"Two men . . . one angry, one regretful." I felt the acid
juices of the one's rage and the other's guilt churning in
my own stomach. "They took turns carrying her body . . .
flung over their shoulders . . . dead weight . . . down to the
river."

"Yes they did," Sal said. "They did, they did."

"No one ever saw Daphne again."

"In the flesh," Sal said.

I felt her hands shake. I squeezed them as I sank
deeper into—I don't know what to call it. Maybe hypno-
sis. I was hypersensitive in a dozen ways: my skin to every
ripple of air, my ears to sounds only animals could pick
up, and my mind to thoughts from some other world.

Now something else was coming through. Grief. "The
tree's really sad because it couldn't protect her, but also
grateful that it could be with her in her final hours, so she
didn't die alone."

"How'd the ear get on the tree?" Gabe asked in a
hushed voice.

I listened, and the story began in the deep, melodic
tones of Timberlarken: *The Africans say if the mind is open,*

all manner of animals, even humans, can speak their hearts to one another. The African girl, Daphne, came to me when I was a sapling. In sorrow and pain, she leaned her head against my reedy trunk. Night after night she leaned on me, seeking solace.

I listened with every fiber of my body, glad to have Sal holding my hands, or I might have melted into the tree.

The blood of her wound bathed my young, green bark. So grateful was I for the nourishment, for the companionship, that I began to heal her ear within my own flesh. I could not give her ear back to her, no, but I could listen for her to every secret of the house. The secrets.

The voice began to fade as a breeze rumbled up, and I strained even harder to hear. Timberlarken's next words wobbled on the wind.

I could not stop those vengeful men in their madness and blood-thirst, but I could hold Daphne in my arms as the life ebbed out of her. And then he came to carry her away.

The voice stopped abruptly.

"Who did?" I asked out loud. I opened my eyes, surprised to find Gabe down from the tree and close enough that I felt his breath on my neck, and Sal's hands locked around my own as if we were joined as one chain. "Who?" I repeated softly, then realized that words from my mouth would not reach Timberlarken as words from my mind would. So I reframed the question: *Who came to carry her away?*

After a long wait, the voice returned. *The one who loved her. He knew that the family meant to cast her into the terrible wilderness of the cotton fields. He could not bear that injustice for his beloved. He knew the oleander just as he knew the birth-*

mark on the back of his hand, as dark as my ancient bark is today.

The voice drifted away again as a truck by the main road roared by.

Silence.

Don't quit on me now!

The Africans say every man and every woman is born to be free as the wind. The man who came to carry Daphne away was born free, but did not die free. His spirit could not rest.

Who? I demanded, frustrated now with Timberlarken's rambling story.

I heard Gabe's voice as if it were coming from the other end of a long tube: "What's he saying, Lila?"

And then I let my sweaty hands slide away from Sal's, sensing that I'd still be linked with the tree. I sank to the ground among Timberlarken's knobby roots.

Look beyond at the man who rakes and rakes, ever trying to clear the leaves and grass for a grave, a comfortable resting place for his beloved, whom he wronged.

The gardener? But why?

Love is a mysterious force. He wished to redeem her from a terrible fate. He meant to sicken the children only slightly, so she could tend them and make them well again, and they would cherish her forever, as he himself did. He never, ever meant for them to die.

Her? Which her?

Even she who is as close to me as the wind and rain. Even the African child, Daphne.

"It wasn't Eulie," I whispered. "It was Luke. He poisoned the Nethercotts."

Sal said, "No kidding, Luke Mullin? So that's why I don't ever see him. He's shamed to show his face to me after all the misery he's caused."

Their voices were distracting, but my connection with Timberlarken was so intense, so sure by that point. *I don't understand . . .*

Do not look for easy answers. Things are not as they seem.

What's not? I demanded, but before an answer came, my concentration was jarred by a car stopping at the Laurel Oaks gates, and suddenly I was whisked back into my own reality—my skin itchy from mosquito bites, my ears bombarded by the beep of the car horn, and my mind hearing only empty silence from Timberlarken.

The blinding sun masked the car, as a shadowy figure got out to open the plantation gates. I heard it's creaking rusty hinges as it gave way to a van.

Gabe said, "It's Mom and Dad. Act normal."

As if we ever could, after what we'd just been through.

Chapter Thirty-nine
Daphne

One time when the house was full of company, way before Birdie went to her rest, Miss Amelia came into the kitchen. Birdie and I were doing up the mountain of dishes, and Miss Amelia whispered, "I may be Yankee-bred, but there's one marvelous Southern custom I certainly cotton to, and it's placing a pineapple on the bedside table of a guest who's stayed too long. Before the day's out, that sojourner will be packing her trunk."

"Yes, ma'am," Birdie and I said, and I could tell she was thinking what I was thinking—*How many pineapples we got out back?*

Well, I'm not ready to stash a pineapple in Lila's room, but in that week of the funeral, when folks lingered on and on, I sure was wishing I had a bushel basket of pine-apples. I sorely needed to get upstairs and take care of Miss Amelia's treasure box, but with the house so full for nine days, and people praying the rosary every time you turned around, and stubby candles burning low in every room, I'd never be able to sneak those *bébés* past the fu-neral callers.

Once we'd seen the last of them, finally, I stayed out of sight of the Judge as much as I could. He was holed up grieving most of the time, and I figured if he didn't see me, maybe he'd soon forget about me. So I hid out in Tante Drucilla's cabin and tended the babies with the old *tantes*, over in what we called the chilluns' house.

Who was I fooling?

First thing, with Alice and Molly and their *maman* in the ground and the guests gone, the Judge closed off the dining room. Said no one was ever to step foot in that room again, and far as I know, no one did until long after, when the Brookes moved their family into this house.

Second thing he did was send for me. Isaac came down to the washline to fetch me to the Judge. *Mon cher* Isaac stood a little apart from us on the back gallery, fussing with a hammer and nails in a loose trellis nearby to give me strength while the Judge—well, I guess you could say he did what his fancy title said—passed judgment on me. I was shaken seeing him up-close. Seemed like he'd lost ten pounds. He sat in one of those rockers while I stood up by him like I'd done a hundred times, but this time was different. All the stuffing'd come out of him, and he couldn't even raise his voice.

"Daphne," he said, flat as a ribbon, and not even looking me in the eye. "I am going to New Orleans for good."

"Yessir." I liked the sound of that, until it passed through my mind: *Well, then, what's to become of all the rest of us?*

"I am closing up the house. Eulie's the only one who'll be staying in it, to keep things tidy until a buyer takes it off my hands. I'll keep the plantation going. Hector will oversee it all, along with Jeb Livingston from over at Aubergine House."

"Yessir." Why was he telling me all this? Found out right quick.

"You may be wondering about your fate, Daphne." Now he looked up, stabbed me with his eyes, and I knew then that his weepy sorrow had hardened into anger same as pure spring water hardens into ice.

"You killed my wife and children."

"Nosir!"

"Don't defy me, Daphne, I am warning you. You will pay. I'd surely be within my rights as a civilized Southern gentleman to have them hang you from a tree until you're dead. Any court of law would decree the same penalty."

Isaac stopped hammering, and for a second I thought he'd raise that hammer to the Judge's head, but he wasn't a foolish man, not Isaac.

The Judge sucked in a huge sigh and barked, "Leave us," and Isaac backed away, flashing me some message. *Be careful? Take heart?* Couldn't read his sweet eyes.

The Judge was saying, "Need I remind you that I own you?"

"Nosir," I whispered.

"I live only for the day I hear your neck snap, hanging from a live oak."

I swallowed, trying not to let my eyes show how scared green I was.

He fanned himself with his hat; the frillies at his collar waved in the breeze while I waited for what came next.

"You won't know when it's coming, Daphne, but you can count on it one of these days while these black clouds are hovering over my house." He fiddled with his earlobe, which was red from his pulling it during all the grieving time. "Meanwhile, the cotton's high. Those fields are just waiting for your labors, Daphne, and Hector will have his eye on you. You already know Hector's might."

"Yessir." I hung my head, feeling that slice of the ear all over again.

"You're of no further use to me in the house, you and your ugly yellow turban. And one more thing, Daphne." He stood up now, just so he could tower over me and make me feel as high as a beetle. "You are never, ever to enter this house again. Do I make myself clear?"

Crazy, my life dangling by a thread, and what did I think about but Miss Amelia's *bébés* upstairs there in her room! I gave her my good word that they'd be hid away until they got into the right hands. Miss Amelia went to her grave believing I'd do the right thing by her, even if she *did* hate me worse than thunder and lightning. But how was I going to get those *bébés* someplace safe like I promised, 'cause, like Miss Amelia once said, every woman might need an escape someday.

"DO I MAKE MYSELF CLEAR?"

"Yessir," I swore, but it was a lie.

The judge waved me off like I was nothing more than a fly buzzing over his head. Soon as I had my back turned, he said, "I'm selling Candlewax to a planter over in Saint James Parish, and the other horses are going to Livingstons'. I won't be needing a livery boy anymore."

I froze in place.

"They need a good stable hand over there in Saint James, so I'm thinking of hiring Isaac out. I'll do better that way than if I'd sell him outright. I expect he won't be back this way for a good long while. You'll be with the worms by then."

I know these words gave the Judge the first joy he'd felt since his family passed, but there wasn't any way I was going to show him how crushed my spirit was right then, and did it really matter if I died? Everyone I loved was gone—Birdie, Alice, Molly, and in a little while Isaac. Even Candlewax, on whose solid hind end Isaac and I had tapped out our future. I took a deep breath and turned around, looked right at the Judge, and said, "That'll be right nice for Isaac, sir. He dotes on that horse. Will that be all, sir?" and I walked away with my head held high 'til I was out of his sight.

Chapter Forty

Lila

Gabe jumped out like a jack-in-the-box. "Hey, Mom and Dad, we're over here, lurking behind the foliage." He turned back to me with a worried frown. "Look at them. I don't think they're ready for this stuff."

"We're not telling them *everything*," I whispered hurriedly.

Dad edged stiffly past the car, with a foam brace that made his neck look about a foot long. I ran over and gently hugged him. "Does it hurt, Dad?"

"Only when I breathe."

Gabe helped Mom out of the car. Half her head and

one eye were bandaged from where she'd bonked herself
against the dashboard, and the other side of her face was a
swollen mass of blue and orange bruises.

I swallowed a sour wad; Mom looked like a war survi-
vor. "Are you sure you should be out of the hospital?"

Dad replied, "We were worried about leaving you kids
here alone, so we skedaddled out of there as quickly as
they'd let us go."

"We'll be okay, really," Mom assured us, wincing with
pain.

"You sure *do* look like you been in a wreck," said Sal.

"Yes, but we're very lucky. It could have been so much
worse." Mom sighed deeply, groping for Dad's hand. "And
who are you, dear?"

"My name's Sal, ma'am. I stay down there in the basement with Miss Camilla, until something better turns up.
It always do, sooner or later."

Gabe said, "Sal's introduced us to real interesting
things around here."

"Yes, ma'am," she said politely. Her eyes darted toward me, then toward Gabe. It seemed she was asking us,
How much should we tell them? I returned her look with a
slight shake of my head, meaning *not much at all.*

"We were just catching some shade in that big old oak
tree out front. No special tree," Sal hurried to add. "Just
some tree."

Mom reared back slowly, which obviously caused her
real pain. "Lila? Is there something we should know?"

"Uh-oh, I done said too much! Happens every time.
Well, I'll be on my way now," Sal said, skipping toward

the root cellar. She turned back and called across the courtyard, "Bye, Yankee girl."

"Be seeing you."

She took a few steps back toward me. "Don't see how, being as you're leaving today, and I never stay put in one place long enough to hardly cast a good shadow." She started backing away again. I followed, and she said, "Give me something of yours, and it'll link us." She murmured under her breath, "Like the tree," Then, for Mom and Dad, "That's what folks used to do, times past. Tie a string around their ankles or some such thing, to keep 'em linked no matter how far apart they got to."

Clueless, Dad said, "Oh, like that song, tie a yellow ribbon 'round the old oak tree."

"Just like that," Gabe replied with a laugh and a glance in my direction.

Mom said, "I sense that I'm missing something."

"Nothing at all!" I assured them.

I could see that Sal was a little nervous, maybe afraid she'd blow our cover. She started inching away again.

"Wait," I said, pulling a silver stud out of my left ear. I felt a gentle jolt of energy as I passed the tiny silver ball to her.

She closed her fingers around it, working it in the palm of her hand. "Uh-huh, this'll do fine," she said, in front of the slanted door down to the dark cellar of the Laurel Oaks house.

I reached out for her. "Wait, Sal. You have to give me something in exchange, or it won't work."

Sal thought a minute, then ripped a button off the

bottom of her shirt. She laughed at the hole it left. "Guess Miss Camilla's gonna have to get out her sewing gear, or send this shirt to the poor box at church, which is probably where she got it anyways." She pressed the yellow button into my hand. "Don't you forget me. You neither, Yankee boy," she called past me.

She opened the cellar door, but I stopped her before she got to the first step. "One more thing I wanted to ask you, Sal."

"Fire away." One of her favorite expressions.

"It's about the General Cambridge Suite."

"What, that room down yonder?" Her eyes darted toward the end of the gallery. "What about it?"

"The welcome letter Camilla left us said we weren't to go into that room. Then when I asked her what was up with the General Cambridge Suite, she got real serious and said it would be revealed to me in good time, not before."

"Sounds like Miss Camilla!" Sal said.

"Well, this is a good time," I insisted.

She perched on the cellar door that seemed like the entrance to a dugout, her chin in the V of her small hands.

"And? So? Tell me right now!"

"Don't know if I should say. Miss Camilla might bust a gasket if she heard."

"Oh, go ahead. The secret's safe with me," I whispered, because I was aware of Mom and Dad back there, talking to Gabe, but watching Sal and me.

Sal swung her feet against the door, *thunk-thunk.* "Lord's honest truth?"

"Absolutely. If the tree tells us the truth, you ought to," I said.

"Yup. Well, there's a real good reason you can't go into the Cambridge place."

"Yes, but what *is* it?" I demanded.

"Lila?" Mom called. "Gabe's talking about a treasure? Maybe you should come back here and tell us what's going on."

"Just a sec, Mom," I called over my shoulder, then turned back to Sal. "Now's the time, quick!"

She giggled, flashing me those crisscross teeth one last time. "It's this, Yankee girl. Toilet overflowed, and the room's a swamp. Smells to high heaven, and I'll bet you there's frogs hopping all over in there. That's the whole mystery!" she said, and she scrambled down the stairs of the root cellar.

I slowly walked back to my family, smiling but not quite ready to break the spell of—whatever it was that Sal and Gabe and I shared, and Timberlarken was part of it, for sure.

My family was huddled around one of the tables, eating the sandwiches Dad had brought back. Crab cake sandwiches. Yuck.

"No hamburger and fries, Dad?" I said with a pout.

"This is seafood territory, Lila. Anyway, I suspect they make their hamburgers from alligator flesh right out of the swamp." He passed me a crab cake sandwich, and I had to admit that it wasn't as gross as I expected.

Dad added, "So, what's this about a treasure? Your brother says you have a lot to tell us. I suggest you start at the beginning."

My eyes shot to Gabe, and he sent me back a silent brother/sister reassurance: *I didn't give them too much yet.*

"Let's go sit up on the gallery," I suggested, fingering the empty hole in my left ear and the button locked in my palm. We took the sandwiches and scooched the rocking chairs into a circle. Funny, those rockers didn't seem nearly as scary as they had two nights earlier. Just chairs. But they were in a circle, and circles had power. That's one thing Laurel Oaks had taught me for sure. So, Gabe and I began to pour out the story—or a version of it. There were things I'd never be able to tell them. Nothing about Luke disappearing before our eyes, or a ghost splitting the storm with an ax. Nothing about a rooster crowing nearly two hundred years after it was dead and dried up. Nothing about Daphne and the mosquito netting and Eulie's spirit in the cat. And certainly nothing about a talking tree named Timberlarken.

Which didn't leave much to tell.

Chapter Forty-one
Daphne

Time was running out, not slow like molasses; pouring like a cloudburst. Didn't know just *what* the Judge had in store for me, but I knew it'd be worse than slicing off my ear, and even worse than setting me out to the cotton fields. Out there worst thing was I'd die of old age before I could even count twenty rings around my trunk, before I even had a husband and *bébé* of my own, but at least I'd be alive 'til I wasn't.

Truth is, some of the folks in the quarters were gloating when the news got down to them that I'd end up in the cotton fields. Most had been out there two, three generations. Had tough old alligator hide tanned by the sun, but I'd worked in the dark, cool of the house the most part of my life. Rowecna wrinkled up her nose like she smelled sour milk every time she felt my hand. All the ladies were jealous, especially leathery old Eulie who couldn't have been more than thirty, though she looked twice that.

Birdie'd shown me how to mix lard with sweet bay gum and rub it in good so my hands and elbows and feet would be as soft as a newborn chick's. I *liked* feeling soft. Maybe I got desperate to stay soft.

Some folks said I'd do anything to keep out of the sun and grime and prickly stalks of the fields, and that's how come my little girls suffered so fierce that last night. Well, it's partway true. I *was* getting mighty scared; felt like Meshach and Abednego in the fiery furnace, about to be licked by the flames. Père Jacques loved telling that story, he did! But I'd swear right to Jesus' face, I'd never, ever do anything to hurt my girls. Lord knows I loved them more than sunshine.

One way or the other, my days were numbered, so I tried to make the best of the ones I had left to me. That last Saturday night, some of the folks called a big sing since it was too hot in the cabins to sleep anyway, and besides that, it was St. John's Eve, celebrating the start of summertime. Over in Baton Rouge and New Orleans, free folks would be dancing all night, and a steamy June night it was, when just sitting on a log made you stew in your own sweat, so we might as well sing out our hearts. We commenced with sad, draggy songs, all of us still mourning Birdie even months after she'd passed. But after a while, like our folks do, we gloried in her going home and took to singing loud and joyful. All that music pulled Luke Mullin out of his shed down yonder, and we spotted him lurking in the shadows, switching his eyes all around. Well, the feeling was running so high that night that Oncle Joe called him right over to join in the ruckus. All of us dancing around a big cauldron cooking a fat snake cut in three, after *Le Père, le Fils, et le Saint-Esprit*. In a minute Luke was clapping and whistling with the rest of us. We were stomping our feet, beating on kettles, and singing loud enough to blow birds right outta the trees:

> *Do Lord, oh do, Lord, oh do remember me . . .*
> and
> *O, who will come and go with me?*
> *I am bound for the promised land . . .*
> and
> *Stand on the rock, stand on the rock,*
> *stand on the rock a little longer . . .*

I had to get up to catch a breeze or I'd of fainted dead away, so I went walking behind Therese and Shem's cabin, and spied Sansant and Eulie's no-good man Anjou having a confab about somebody. Heard, "She's getting too big for her britches. Ast me, I'd say somebody need to take her down a rung or two. Ifn she ain't wake up dead first, she gonna bring trouble down on all our heads."

"Maybe we be able to hide her somewheres." That was Sansant talking, and not too convincing.

Who could they be jawing about? Most probably Eulie, I was thinking, and her own man Anjou talking that way about her! Well, you know how it goes. I hid behind the necessary and watched and listened, my good ear sharpened to their spitfire words.

"Tante Drucilla got her now, but don't plan on her hiding down here too many more days, Sansant. Judge so mad with her for what she done to his wife and babies, he want her dead and cold. Heard Hector and him talking about it."

I was starting to suspicion who they meant, and it wasn't Eulie.

Scared me to the very blood pounding under my skin to realize *she* and *her* was me, and that whenever the Judge sent me down, those two (and how many others, I don't know) weren't about to let me see the next sunrise. With Birdie gone and Isaac about to be hired away, who was going to stop them? Not Tante Drucilla. She already had one foot in heaven. That left nobody at all.

I had nowhere to turn, neither. Didn't know who my friends were anymore. I crept away from the singing party. Only one saw me go was Luke Mullin. He tipped his floppy white hat, saying, "Good evening, Miss Daphne." I barely nodded and swished my skirt by him, heading for my tree.

I leaned my good ear into Timberlarken's trunk all rough against my cheek. I heard him running with sap, like a pump priming to give cold, sweet water.

"What'll I do?" I whispered, moaning, too.

Be brave, Daphne. Turn to me for comfort.

"Some comfort, when I'm dead and in the ground. Scares me to think of them throwing dirt over me down inside that pine box."

They will not lay you in the ground, Daphne.

"You promising? And what about *mon cher* Isaac? He just gave up his *maman*, and then what'll happen to him when I've passed over?"

The young African is a valuable commodity. It has been decided. He is to be sold off.

"No, hired away close by, in St. James Parish. He'll be back before I know it."

No, Daphne. He will be sold deep into Alabama, along with the prized stallion. All of the Africans will be sold soon after. Then Judge Nethercott will leave here, never to return. You must warn them. Go at once to say good-bye to the young African you love.

I jumped to my feet and ran to the stables with tears pouring like rain down my face. Isaac was surprised to see me, in the light of day.

"He's fixing to sell you off," I cried to Isaac.

"I guessed it, Miss Daphne. Candlewax, too?"

"You both."

"And he's plannin' worse, for you." His voice was sad and low, like it was floating around in his throat. He looked away, combed Candlewax until her hair stood up flyaway, and she whinnied in pleasure.

"What'll we do?" I wailed. Candlewax turned around to look at me. She nuzzled up against Isaac, and I don't know, maybe she whispered to him.

"Nothing I can do now, Miss Daphne. Some's got

power, some don't. Lay your hand on this horse's rump, same as we always do. Firm and solid, like you and me together."

I did, and he put his hand over mine. "I'll think on it. Now scat, Miss Daphne, before you get caught where you ain't s'pose to be."

Middle of the night, I crept back into the house. The Judge was snoring in his room across from Miss Amelia's, and why they couldn't of shared a room, I don't know. Eulie, she'd be moving right into Alice's old room, soon as the Judge left, bold hussy that she was. No sleeping behind the stove for that one. Meanwhile, I had to creep by her, thankful for her snuffly snoring.

All the rest of the house was heavy with emptiness and grief. I tiptoed up the stairs, scared at every creak. Didn't dare carry a candle, afraid the Judge might see the light flickering from under his door. Felt my way in the dark along the wall to Miss Amelia's room. Slipped in there and dropped to the floor at the side of the bed and pulled out that fancy leather box. Her *bébés* were just as heavy as I remembered. Got the key, too, from her Emporium hatbox.

I couldn't take the chance of getting caught with that thing in my hands, if the Judge might need to go to the necessary in the dark of night, so I made a sling out of a bedsheet from Miss Amelia's linen chest, and tied that leather box to my own self. Raised the window sash. Anchored down like I was with the *bébés*, I crawled right out onto the eaves and down the side of the house on a drain pipe until it was just a little jump to the ground. Hurt like anything because my ankle wasn't all healed up from when the Judge stomped me, but I got away.

Down at the stable, I pulled the heavy door open by the brass ring.

"Isaac?" I whispered. "You in here?"

His sleepy voice came out of the darkness. "Uh huh, over here, Miss Daphne."

I saw a dark shadow grow into a full-sized man, and when my eyes got used to the dark, I saw his face clear. Missed him already, and he wasn't even gone.

I gave Isaac the box with Miss Amelia's *bébés* and made him promise to hide it where the Judge would never find it.

"I know just where, Miss Daphne. Mama Birdie showed me the safest place in the whole house. It's inside of a wall in that north room up top of the stairs. Nobody gonna look there for a hundred years."

"How are you gonna get in the house? The Judge sure won't throw the door open to you."

"You gotta trust me to find some means. I'll use Eulie, if I have to. And I'ma kill me a rooster in the moonlight tonight and hide his head in there for keeping it all safe, just like Mama Birdie would of. And that rooster, he ain't crowing 'til the rightful folks come along."

"I sure wish Birdie was here," I whispered, my heart near breaking for losing *mon cher* Isaac, too.

He put his arm around me, kind of stiff-like, not pulling me too close. Said, "Tomorrow before the wagon come for me and Candlewax, I'ma take care of it for you. You got my promise, Miss Daphne."

He never asked what was inside the leather box. Didn't have to. Isaac and me, we trusted each other all together. Isn't that how love's s'pose to be?

"I'm never gonna see you again," I said.

"Not 'til the next world, Miss Daphne, better world." He took my small hand in his big one and pulled me down to sit beside him. Except for when he went out after that rooster, he stayed next to me all the rest of the night long, slantdickelar up against a bale of hay, me sleeping with my head on his sharp-boned shoulder, and Candle-wax keeping an eye on us same as Birdie would of.

Chapter Forty-two

Lila

Here's what we told Mom and Dad.

"It must be the power of suggestion," Gabe began. "But some people around this place see things that aren't exactly there."

"Like what?" Mom asked quickly.

I glanced at Gabe. "Oh, like we went on the candlelight tour the first night, while you guys were asleep, and Camilla told us about somebody who died at the front door. I sort of saw the outline of his body."

"Power of suggestion," Gabe said again. "It's the same guy who was supposed to have died on the twelfth step after some ride-by shooting thing in the 1880s. Remember? The management warned us in that hokey note."

"What else?" Dad wore a worried frown. He planted his shoes firmly on the floor to put a break on the rocker.

"Um, a mirror cracked," I began.

"Seven years bad luck," said Mom with a pained smile. She motioned toward her bruises and bandages.

I said, "There were a lot of rooster crowings, even in the middle of the day. And mysterious lights that twinkled and disappeared. Sal says they're called swamp lights." Actually, that's the one weird thing that we *didn't* see, so I thought it would throw them off the track. Gabe picked up on it right away.

"Those swamp lights are supposed to lead the way to a treasure, at least that's what Louisiana people believe."

Mom attempted another smile, which obviously hurt her face. "Yes, Gabe started to tell us about some treasure. What did you find?"

Gabe's eyebrows were raised in a *what now?* expression, and I said, "He'll tell you about it."

"Yeah," he began, stalling for time. "Well, we found something hidden in Lila's room, behind an ugly antique needlepoint thing."

"What was it?" Mom's one visible eye was opened wide, probing for information to make sense of this stuff.

I said, "It's fabulously valuable. Gold, encrusted with diamonds and rubies and emeralds and jade. Gabe, go up and get it."

Usually he didn't take orders from me, since I was the bossiest member of the Barry family, but this time he said,

"Okay. I've gotta go pack my gear anyway if we're leaving right after lunch." He left his rocking chair banging against the wooden deck as he rocketed into the house.

While he was upstairs, I filled Mom and Dad in on more details. "It's a pair of cherubs, twins. We think they represent the mistress of this house, and her twin sister, who died at birth." As I said it, that clammy feeling of the Ophelia Raye baby filled me, as if I'd touched a body in a casket. I must have turned pale.

Mom reached out to me. "Lila? Are you all right?"

"Just thinking. We're not sure how the statue got there, but those cherubs seem to hold some important secret. I have a feeling Gabe and I were meant to find them and unravel the mystery." I didn't mention Daphne, the mosquito netting, *find the babies in the wall* . . .

"I see, and I suppose they whispered their secret to you?" Dad said, as if he didn't believe a word of any of this.

"No, the cherubs didn't talk to me," I replied, trying to think fast. "There was a letter under their feet, in Mrs. Nethercott's own handwriting, about how she and her two daughters were poisoned. We didn't absolutely know who committed the murder."

"Murder?" Mom cried. "Oh, mercy, Ethan."

Dad patted her hand. "Let's just listen," he said quietly.

"Well, we think it was a murder," I hedged, "or it could have been an accident. We just didn't know who did it until—" I stopped, convinced that Mom and Dad should never know about Timberlarken.

"Until?" Mom repeated.

"Until a caretaker told us the ancient truths." Timber-larken *was* a caretaker, though not the kind Mom would understand.

"Not a ghost, but a living caretaker. That's a relief." Mom had her hand over her heart.

Depends on how you define "living," I thought.

Gabe was back with the cherubs, then. He stood the hefty little statue up on the arm of Dad's chair.

"Breathtaking," Mom said, "and who does this belong to?"

"That's debatable," Gabe answered.

Mom ran her finger over the gold mesh scales, the lacy wings, the diamond-studded toes. "It's quite beautiful, in an ornate, overdone, gaudy way. Ethan, what do you think the kids should do with it?"

I recognized this trick. It was the game called *we-parents-know-the-answer-and-now-we're-waiting-for-you-children-to-discover-it-on-your-own.*

"Sell it to somebody filthy rich," Gabe suggested. "Bill Gates, maybe, or J. K. Rowling."

"A possibility," Dad said, which meant *fat chance!* "We could send it to Sotheby's to auction," he suggested. "The kids would have to give the auction house a commission, but they'd still have enough left over to pay for all of their college."

"That's a viable option," Mom agreed. Translation: *forget it—no way on earth.*

My recommendation: "We could take turns keeping it in our rooms. Or get a glass case for it and plunk it on our mantel for company to admire, and then they'd have to ask where it came from, and we'd tell them the whole story, with us as stars." Not the *whole* story.

"Hmmn, that would be enthralling," said Mom.

Dad added, "If we kept it on our mantel, the insurance would be prohibitive." He lifted the statue and turned it on his palm. "This little trinket is worth more than our whole house. Any other ideas?"

There was only one answer Dad was looking for, and reluctantly I uttered it like a giant concession: "I know, I know, we give it to the owner."

"Which is the historical society that runs Laurel Oaks," Dad added. "And maybe it'll be displayed in that little museum in town."

Along with Amelia's letter, I thought, and then everyone will know Daphne's innocent after 170 years. I was warming to the idea, although I hated giving up the babies that Daphne had worried over for so long.

"All right, let's all pack up and go to the Bide-a-Wee Motel in town," Dad said, gingerly sliding to his feet. "First thing tomorrow we'll stop at the historical museum on our way home. This will certainly knock them for a loop."

Dad-talk. Absolutely nobody said things like *knock them for a loop,* but then nobody got keyed up over muffulettas and crab cakes like Dad.

Now Mom asked, "So, kids, what would you tell the people at the museum if they wanted to offer you a reward? After all, you've made a significant contribution to the lore of Laurel Oaks, and you're giving them a priceless piece of their history. It's not unreasonable to expect a reward of some kind."

"Not money," Dad quickly added.

Before I could reply, Gabe insisted, "We've gotta make them display these babies with a plaque that has our names on it as the investigative reporters." He etched our names in the air: "Gabriel Garrison Barry and, oh yeah, that other anonymous person, Lila Somebody."

"Thanks," I muttered, giving him a good-natured punch. "Here's what I'd ask for. Nobody remembers who Maude Eberly was, or Samuel Gladstone. They're the ones the rooms upstairs are named for. But if the museum renamed the rooms and posted the incredible adventures of Lila and Gabriel Barry, we'd be remembered forever."

"Makes us sound like an old married couple," Gabe groused.

"We'll work on the wording, kids. Meanwhile, it's an excellent idea," Dad agreed.

"Oh, one little bitty detail." Here goes, I thought. They're going to ground me until I'm thirty. "We sort of owe the historical society for the mirror we broke."

"And the antique needlepoint needs to be repaired," Gabe added. "But that's minor stuff, compared to Lila's original plan, which was to hack the wall with an ax."

"I never said that!"

"Don't worry, kids, we'll settle with the historical society and just deduct it from your allowances for the next ten years," Dad threatened, with mischief in his eyes. "Anything else we should know?"

Plenty! "No, not really," I said casually, and Gabe stomped my foot under the table.

"Well, it's been quite a vacation," Dad said. He patted Mom's knee.

"Aren't you glad we were only gone twenty-four hours, Ethan? In another day they'd have sold the state of Louisiana back to the French."

Dad smiled. "All right, Barry family, we've got to hit the road. We'll all go up and get our things. Gabe, Mom and I will need some help, and Lila, no woo-woo shenanigans, you hear? Halloween's not for a couple of weeks yet."

Chapter Forty-three
Daphne

When Isaac's wagon was just a speck way off, I sat right down in the dusty road and cried my eyes red. I remembered about Alice saying one night while I brushed her hair a hundred strokes, like she liked, "Daphne, you are just my very best friend in the whole world." And Molly running to the back of the church to my open arms, after her *maman* scolded her for dropping her hymnal in the baptizing fountain. And Birdie teaching me about manure and tree talking. She never could stay mad at me, even after that bad thing I did with the gris-gris bag.

And Isaac. I knew I'd never see *mon cher* again 'til we were with the saints.

But you know how it goes. You can't feel sorry for yourself for long, or you'd be wallowing like pigs in mud. So, I picked my own self up, dusted me off, and headed to the chilluns' house down in the quarters to take care of the little ones for the last day. Next morning, I'd be out picking cotton at sunup, from can-see to can't-see, with Hector's mean eyes watching me all the time, until every bone in my body would be crying for the comfort of one of Birdie's secret remedies, or until the worst came to me when I wasn't looking.

I remember the prickly grass and leaves under my bare feet, and summer leaves dried up, and Luke Mullin raking them into crunchy piles. And smoke and meaty smells pouring out of the smokehouse, and the sky a clear, cloudless blue the color of my Alice's eyes. Those are the pictures I keep in my mind, because what happened next, I don't want to remember, but I can't disremember.

Anjou and Sansant came 'round on their lunch break. I can still hear their tin cups rattling against their pails.

"She's right there!" Anjou cried, and they both rushed toward me. I couldn't of outrun them if I'd tried, so I stayed planted where I was.

"You ain't nothing but trouble," Sansant said. "Judge have it in for you, and he leaving it to us to do the job. Ain't nothing personal."

"Sure is," said Anjou, Eulie's no-good man. "She done got all stuck up in that fine house, and killed them little white girls dead. If that ain't personal, I don't know what is."

"Grab her feet," Sansant said. He wrestled me to the ground with my hands behind my back and my face in the dry grass and sent Anjou for rope. Sansant just sat right on me, his knees around my waist, like I was a horse fit for riding.

My blood was pounding in my head, so I almost missed his whispers in my good ear. "Hector gonna string us up ourselves if we don't do this, Miss Daphne. I got a young one to think about. I'm real sorry."

In a minute, Anjou came back with a length of rope. They hog-tied me and dragged me through the grass to where the tall oaks stood. I heard Luke Mullin raking and raking the same piles, but even if he'd of lifted that rake and dug its teeth into either Anjou or Sansant, one, the other would have done me in and Luke Mullin besides.

I looked up from the ground at a sky full of trees, dreading and hoping that they'd pick the one I knew best. They did. Prayed my tree would save me—drop a huge branch on their heads maybe, or draw lightning to them but it didn't happen.

I knew what was coming. Let myself go limp, my mind, too, and gave myself over to Timberlarken. If I was going home, it'd be in the arms of my last friend in the world.

Can't talk about that part, or when Luke Mullin came and got me down, or when those others let me sink to the bottom of the Mississippi. Got to think on what happened this afternoon. How that Lila and Sal and Gabriel scratched out the truth, sending me home to Jesus free and clear, and it's about time that happened. Up 'til then, I wasn't sure if maybe I *did* poison my girls, without knowing just how. Hard to surprise an old soul like me, but I tell you, that letter inside with the beautiful golden *bébés*, it really caught me up. I always knew it wasn't me on purpose who did the poisoning. Now if I see Birdie one of these days, I can look her in the eye and say it wasn't me by accident, neither.

Well, I sure wasn't any good with the whammies and healings—Birdie'd be the first to tell you that—but I'd picked up enough from her to know that a few crumbs of crushed oleander petals or a few drops of its sap sprinkled over the cake while we were running every which way fixing Molly's birthday supper was all it would take to send a body right to *alléluia* land.

Luke, all along, imagine. He's the one, and I'm not, and not Eulie, neither. Glory be! I'm free now, just like *ma mère*, Henriette, always dreamed for me.

This old house is going to quiet down now that Eulie's gone for good. And she is. I saw that cat run right across the road. I'm praying she's over to Aubergine House haunting the Livingstons' kinfolks, or at the Greeks'. Luke Mullin, rest his soul, I hope he's put down his rake and gone home to his shed down close to the river to take up that book he was always reading. Reading it since way back in *those* times. You'd think he'd of finished it by now.

Lila and them are leaving, too. Sure will be lonesome. Sal's still here, though, and that gives us who're left some promise when all those rubbernecking folks come looking for a cold-chill, trying to catch us used-to-bes on their machines.

I don't know if others from different times in Laurel Oaks' doings are still around, but if they are, they're no account, 'cause they don't even have names, and a spirit without a name, well now, it's just an empty peanut shell with no nugget inside.

Like my ear—there but not *there*.

I put my hand to that ugly scar in my mind, and what do I find? A whole nice brown ear, soft and cushiony. I won't be needing that yellow turban anymore, now that I'm whole again.

Timberlarken's welcoming me home now. I'm chewing down what fear's kept me away so I can rest my weary soul curled up here on Timberlarken's branch. Way up here, I might could see Molly and Alice, maybe even Birdie.

There just has to be some kind of good that comes from bumping around a place as long as I've been, and here's what I know now that I didn't know back then. Heaven isn't a place like Tante Drucilla promised, a mansion of many rooms with featherbeds and harp-string music fit to soothe the soul. And it's not fluffy clouds holding you up and floating you around for all eternity. Unh-uh. Heaven's just whatever you need it to be.

Someday Isaac will find his way to me and bring me those wildflowers he picked that sad, terrible day of Molly's birthday. And me and *mon cher* Isaac will nest there forever and a day, high up in my tree, our own slice of heaven.

Chapter Forty-four

Lila

We all went into the house to pack, but as soon as I could slip away, I ran outside to say good-bye to Timberlarken. There was no need to circle the tree anymore. We heard each other clearly from my first touch of his rough bark.

My family and I are leaving in a minute. Leaving. I'd never noticed how close that word was to leaves.

It will be lonesome here without you.

Tears clouded my eyes. I leaned my forehead toward the tree.

He said, *There is more to tell.*

Yes?

Things are not as they seem.

You told me that already. I tried to be patient, but I didn't want Mom and Dad to find out that I wasn't in my room.

Timberlarken understood the urgency and poured his story out quickly in disjointed words and thoughts. *Daphne's sweetheart Isaac had no choice . . . he trusted Eulie . . . upstairs in the north room . . . he opened the wall . . . could not resist looking in the box, Pandora's box . . .*

I remembered something about Pandora's box from a story we read in English, how it held the troubles of the world that spilled out when she lifted the lid.

. . . found the letter . . . read a few words . . .

Isaac could read?

A few words only, learned from a wise teacher, Uncle Joe, who read little but secretly taught everything he knew to Isaac . . . He recognized her name.

Whose? Daphne's?

Not Daphne's. Eulie's . . . enough other words to grasp the meaning. He told her . . . her fear knew no bounds . . . both thought the letter gave the truth . . . that Eulie poisoned them.

She did it? I thought it was Luke.

She did not, but Isaac could not read all the words . . . the ones about the gardener . . .

And Daphne?

Timberlarken shuddered; his leaves shook. *She paid for the gardener's deeds . . . Eulie as well . . . went to her death believing she was responsible.*

Timberlarken had one last thing to say to me: *The*

*distant drums you hear from this day forward will be of two
kinds, Indian and African. Listen.*

And then we were both silent.

I ran upstairs and stuffed everything into my suitcase and
backpack. Gabe came in, toting his gear, and said, "One
last look around. Let's remember every single detail, because we'll never have an experience like this again in our
whole lives. If we're lucky."

"Gabe, you have to promise me something. It's about
Timberlarken. Absolutely no one hears about him. Not
Mom, not Dad, and none of your band or baseball bud-
dies, either. Timberlarken is a secret that stays here at
Laurel Oaks."

"I can't promise that."

"You have to!"

"But, Lila, don't you see? If we take the cherubs and the
letter to the museum, people still won't know who poisoned
the Nethercotts. Reading the letter, you'd wonder, was it
Eulie? Was it Luke? Think about it, we really don't know for
sure."

"I know everything now. Timberlarken shared all the
secrets with me."

"I figured you'd go back before we pulled out of this
place."

"It's Luke, no question. We know for sure," I said thought-
fully, "and everyone else who reads the letter will know, at
least, that Daphne was innocent. Gabriel Barry, Scout's
honor: Timberlarken's name is *never* mentioned once we
leave here, swear?"

"Yeah, I'll give it a try, but no promises."

I wrapped the cherubs in my nightshirt and stuffed the bundle into my suitcase. We opened the door. "Are you surprised to see that the hall light's on again?"

"Not anymore. Camilla probably comes up here and unscrews the bulb a dozen times a week. She's a fake, not even a good one."

"But Sal's the real thing," I said.

Gabe jammed the zipper on his duffel, and he was wrestling with it to get the teeth back on track.

"You're hopeless. Let me do it," I said, grabbing it away from him. One-two, I had it sliding like it had been greased.

"You're way too aggressive for a girl."

"A girl can't ever be too aggressive," I shot back, shoving his bag into the hall.

He had his sports gear hanging off one shoulder, his trombone off the other, and his perfect hair hanging over one eye as usual. My brother.

We took one last look around the Maude Eberly room. The Fragrant Rose sampler tilted on the wall, still refusing to hang straight.

"It's over now, Gabe. They're gone, Daphne and Eulie both, I know it. Luke, too. I miss them, don't you?"

"We'll be staying in a boring old motel tonight, and, yeah, I'll miss the action here."

"Hold on, I can't remember if I packed my cell."

Gabe reached for my backpack.

"Don't touch it. You'll jam it like you did your duffel."

I knelt in the hall to unzip my bag—and saw something

that sent my heart hammering wildly. "Gabe, come here!" My hands shook as I touched the item lying on top of my iPod. It was vaguely familiar: an old, worn, threadbare, lopsided, sweat-stained yellow . . . hat.

Daphne's turban.

Epilogue

Daphne and Lila Together

"Listen . . ."

A Note from the Author

Fact? Truth? Fiction? Myth?

Imagine a long rope. Fact holds one end and Fiction holds the other. They're having a friendly debate about what's true and what's not, taking a step back with each point they score, until the rope is pulled taut.

Myth is what totters on the tightrope between Fact and Fiction.

Because so much of *The Secret of Laurel Oaks* is based on fact, and so much of it is *true,* but not factual, I think it's important that you have some clues as to what's historical, what's legend, and what I made up.

All the dialogue and character traits are my invention,

and so is Laurel Oaks Plantation. However, it's closely based on a mysterious place called Myrtles Plantation, which really exists in St. Francisville, Louisiana. Though Myrtles is no longer a working plantation, the gracious home is owned by a private family and not the historical society, as in my story. The owners welcome overnight guests and offer candlelight tours that are spooky and enthralling.

The house was built in 1794 on a Tunica Indian burial site, which might account for some of the odd things that have happened on the grounds. Most of what I describe in my story comes directly from the lore of Myrtles.

My characters, Judge Clark Nethercott and Amelia Maye Nethercott, are modeled after Judge Clark Woodruffe (sometimes spelled Woodruff) and his wife, Sara Matilda, who actually lived. They had two young daughters, possibly a third, but the children's names have been lost to history. In this story, I've given them the names Alice and Molly. After a birthday dinner in the 1830s, history affirms, the two girls and Mrs. Woodruffe met an excruciating death from poison.

Now, about Daphne. Both history and legend tell us that one of the slaves at Myrtles was a girl named Chloe. She worked as a trusted house servant and became a great favorite of the Woodruffes, for various reasons. The story goes that she eavesdropped on a private conversation between the Judge and Mrs. Woodruffe, and as punishment, the Judge ordered her ear sliced off. Ever after, she wore a green turban to hide the ugly scar. Obviously, my character, Daphne, is Chloe in thin disguise.

The myth about Chloe—what totters between fact and fiction—is that she poisoned the Woodruffes, but why she might have done it is open to speculation. Some people say she was afraid of being cast out of the house into the much harsher life of the cotton fields and slave quarters. In desperation, they say, she sprinkled a few crumbs of deadly oleander leaves into the birthday cake batter, intending to make the girls just a little sick. Then she would heroically cure them and prove herself indispensable to the household. Others say Chloe poisoned the family out of vengeance for Judge Woodruffe's heartless treatment of her. Either way, she couldn't have suspected that three people would die that night.

Whichever motive makes the most sense to you (and maybe neither does), the story continues that she was thrown out of the house, into the arms of others down in the slave quarters. Remember, slaves lived under terrible, terrorizing conditions. Plantation owners conspired to strip them of their dignity, freedom, and power. Each step they took could bring severe punishment, even death. So, the slaves at Myrtles feared for their own lives if they did not follow the Judge's barbaric orders to carry out justice as he decreed it. Thus, people who were once her friends hanged Chloe from a tree on the plantation and delivered her body into the murky depths of the Mississippi River.

A few words about conjure, also called *voudoun,* voo-doo, hoodoo, and mojo, as practiced by slaves. It was (still is) a mystical craft growing out of the traditional African belief that all things, living and dead, have spirits, and certain people have the ability to communicate with those spirits. Tree talking was one such gift that could be developed by a sensitive person who was open to voices from beyond the human realm.

The conjure arts became a way to tame the chaos of slavery and return to kidnapped Africans and their descendants the power over their own days and destinies that had been stolen from them. The fixes, hexes, charms, and whammies described in this novel are based on extensive research and careful reading of hundreds of slave narratives and interviews. Whether these whammies caused bizarre happenings or cured dreaded diseases is open to interpretation. What's key is that many black and white people of the time *believed* such feats were true, and therefore they worked. Mind over matter, or magic? You'll have to decide.

So, you know what's fact, and what's myth. Now, here's what's at the fiction end of the rope. All the other characters in both the contemporary and historical portions of the story are made-up. Lila and Gabe, Sal and Camilla; Luke, Birdie, Isaac, Eulie, Tante Drucilla, Oncle Joe, the twin cherubs, and all the rest spring from my imagination.

While I was walking the tightrope of Chloe's legend, something unexpected turned up. That's the joy of writing stories; they surprise the author at every bend. What happened is that I started to love Chloe, and it's hard for us to believe that people we love could do terrible things. I came to see her not as a villain, but as a heroically tragic victim. Novels are based on *what if*. So I wondered, what if someone *else* poisoned the Woodruffes, but Chloe was unfairly blamed, and even today, 170 years later, people still brand her as a heartless murderer? Wouldn't her soul wander restlessly for eons until the truth came out? And what of all the other ghosts that haunt Myrtles Plantation? No fewer than ten murders and suicides are said to have occurred on these splendid grounds. Don't those souls deserve some peace, also?

One September eleventh, which happens to be my birthday, my husband and I stayed at the Myrtles. I'm happy to report no poisoned birthday cake! However, we were truly the only people at the house that night. We wandered the grounds freely. One tree in particular beckoned to us, and we hovered near it during the dark, eerie night, listening for Chloe's voice.

In the light of the next day, we saw something remarkable about that tree. High up, the trunk bore a huge pink scar in the unmistakable shape of an ear. This is the absolute truth. Chills rippled down our spines, and the story began to gather words in my mind. Since that day, I haven't been able to chase the image of the Ear Tree from my mind.

Is Myrtles Plantation haunted? Many swear they've heard and felt and seen a whole panoply of ghosts at the house. In fact, the Myrtles is on the Smithsonian Institution's list of the ten most haunted houses in America, and for good reason. Some report seeing the ghost of a graceful French ballerina. Others have spotted the Woodruffe girls perched on the roof, or bouncing on beds, while still others report mysterious piano music or waking to a face peering at them through parted mosquito netting.

The mirror in the entrance hall actually has been re-placed nine times, and the splotch like dripping blood reappears each time. Some people see Chloe's image in the mirror. Arguably the most persuasive evidence? A strange, indistinct photo of an old-fashioned turbaned figure standing between two Myrtles buildings. The photographer was convinced he'd captured Chloe's ghost on film.

Finally, the antique needlepoint sampler bearing the poem "Fragrant Is the Rose" does, in fact, hang on the wall at Myrtles, in the Fannie Williams room. For this story the room is renamed the Maude Eberly. What's behind the sampler, I cannot say.

Why not go and see for yourself?

About the Author

Lois Ruby spent one night at the haunted Myrtles Plantation in St. Francisville, Louisiana. Her experiences there inspired her to write *The Secret of Laurel Oaks*. A former librarian, Ms. Ruby is the author of several popular books for young readers, including the successful historical novel *Steal Away Home*. She lives in Albuquerque, New Mexico, with her husband. You can find out more about her on her Web site at www.loisruby.com.

The Secret of Laurel Oaks
Lois Ruby

•

ABOUT THIS GUIDE

The information, activities, and discussion questions that follow are intended to enhance your reading of *The Secret of Laurel Oaks*. Please feel free to adapt these materials to suit your needs and interests.

WRITING AND RESEARCH ACTIVITIES

I. *Ghost Stories*

A. Go to the library or go to the Internet to find literary definitions for *fact, fiction, myth, legend, folk tale*, and *ghost story*. Reread the author's note in which she defines *myth* as "what totters on the tightrope between Fact and Fiction." Write a short essay in which you explain your own understanding of the relationship between fact and fiction, using some of the terms defined above. If desired, invite friends or classmates to read their essays aloud. Are your essays similar, or is there a great variety of ways people understand the interplay between fact and fiction?

B. Individually or in small groups, create an illustrated bibliography of your favorite ghost stories and other mysterious tales. Or, write a letter to a friend or classmate, recommending *The Secret of Laurel Oaks* or another spooky story.

C. Take an online trip to the Myrtles Plantation (www.myrtles plantation.com), the Winchester House (www.winchestermystery house.com), the Bell Witch Farm in Adams, Tennessee (www .bellwitch.org), or another famous haunted building. Write a short, illustrated report about the building's architecture, history, and ghost-related lore.

D. Divide friends or classmates into groups to research (1) the history of landmark buildings in your city, town, or state, and (2) local or state legends or ghost stories. Have each group fill a container with index cards each containing a single interesting fact from their research (enough for the entire class). Take turns drawing one card from the HISTORY container and one card from the LEGEND container. Each student must use the information drawn from their cards, plus other research as desired, and their imagination to write a ghost story. Collect the stories in a class book, entitled *The Secrets Of* [your town or state].

II. Language and Culture
A. Daphne incorporates French words that became part of the language of Louisiana slaves. List italicized French words and phrases from the story. Find their English definitions. Create a short translation guide to help readers of this story. How does this incorporation of French language affect your reading of the novel?

B. Go to the library or go to the Internet to learn about the history of Jemez Pueblo, its people's encounters with Spanish conquistadors and with other Native American groups, and the nation and its culture as they exist today. Make an informative poster based on your research.

C. Research Louisiana Creole culture. How has the term *Creole* been applied to different groups in Louisiana, including West African slaves such as Daphne? Research and prepare a Creole recipe, such as dirty rice, to share with family, friends, or classmates. Can you determine the African influences to the recipe? What other cultures and cuisines are represented in your dish? Does your family prepare foods that reflect your cultural background? Bring in a recipe or prepared dish to share with friends or classmates, explaining its importance to your family as a link between your current home state and country and your family's heritage.

D. In the character of Lila, write a journal entry or short essay describing any similarities you sense in her relationship with Roberto's world and with Daphne's.

III. *Between Worlds*

A. Daphne, Eulie, and the other ghosts have been caught between the worlds of the living and the dead. Imagine you are a professor of "ghost science." Using details from the novel, give a "lecture" to friends or classmates explaining why and how these ghosts have been trapped and what will set them free. If desired, dress as you imagine a ghost expert would and offer to answer questions at the end of your presentation.

B. In the character of Eulie, Miss Amelia, Molly, or Alice, write a short essay or journal entry describing what it is like to be trapped between worlds. Or use chalk, colored pencils, or other arts materials to draw a picture of one of these character's ghosts haunting Laurel Oaks.

C. In the character of the living Daphne, write a short speech about feeling how you belong neither with the Nethercott family nor the field-worker slaves. Perform your speech for friends or classmates.

D. The laurel tree is an important image in the novel as it has often been throughout history and legends. Go to the library or go to the Internet to learn more about laurels as examined through many lenses, such as botanical science, history, literature, and mythology. On a large sheet of paper, sketch a laurel tree and surround its branches with facts learned from your research.

E. What worlds do Lila and Gabe move between? Pueblo and Anglo? Music and sports? Believing in ghosts and not believing? In the character of Lila or Gabe, write a letter to a friend back home, describing how you feel caught between worlds or ideas.

DISCUSSION QUESTIONS

1. The novel is framed by one word: *listen*. What are some positive and negative ideas the novel associates with this word? To what or whom are story characters advising readers to listen? Why is it important to listen in your own life?

2. What does the prologue reveal to readers about Daphne? What mysteries or questions do you want answered after reading these opening pages? What images or story elements from the opening chapters are revisited throughout, or at the end of,

the novel? How does this give the novel a special rhythm, perhaps a drumlike syncopation?

3. In the first chapter, how does Lila explain her family's arrival
at Laurel Oaks, and why has her desire to stay there changed
since the trip was planned? What are Lila, Gabe, and their parents' differing reactions to Laurel Oaks in the early chapters of
the novel?

4. Does this story feel like a "ghost story" from the start? What
ideas, images, or literary elements make it feel like a ghost story
to you? Does Daphne's use of Louisiana French terms, such as
bébé and *mon cher*, add a mysterious quality to the novel? How
does the weather add an unusual quality to the story?

5. Who is Sal? Do you believe she is simply helping to create a
spooky atmosphere at Laurel Oaks for visitors, or do you agree
with Lila that she, too, sees ghosts? What is important about
Lila's friendship with Sal? How does Sal help lead Lila and Gabe
to important clues to solving the mystery?

6. What is oleander? What ominous introduction do readers get
to this flower in chapter 2? What does Birdie explain about uses
of oleander in the course of the story? How do other elements of
houdoun (voodoo) permeate the novel?

7. In chapter 13, Lila describes being pulled back from the
Christmastime dancing at the Jemez Pueblo by her mother, who
tells her it is "not for Anglos." How does this incident help you
understand Lila? Do you think her ability to understand being
an outsider helps her connect with Daphne? In what ways is
Daphne also an outsider? What other characters from Daphne's
and Lila's stories struggle with a feeling of being an outsider
and how does this affect them?

8. The story is told in alternating viewpoints, Daphne's and Lila's.
Compare and contrast the Daphne and Lila chapters in terms of
the girls' voices, especially the way they mourn death and think
of those who have died.

9. Describe at least three ways in which food plays an important role in both modern day and historical chapters. Does food
help your family connect with its culture, invoke special mem-
ories, or play other important roles in your life? Describe these
roles.

10. What does Lila come to realize is the true story of the deadly history of Laurel Oaks? Who do you think is most guilty and/ or most responsible for the deaths: Mrs. Nethercott, Luke, or Eulie? Do you think Judge Nethercott or other characters bear some of the responsibility for the events of that tragic night? Why or why not?

11. Do you believe in ghosts? In the ability of certain people to connect to the past or to objects in nature, such as Timberlarken? Do ghostly souls need to be put to rest by truths set free or by other means? Explain your answers and, if you have ever had an experience you felt had a ghostly quality, describe it.

12. How can *The Secret of Laurel Oaks* be read not just as a ghost story but as a tale about walking between different cultures, different worlds, and even between the literary poles of fact and fiction? What insights can readers draw about understanding differences from reading this novel?